A DIFFERENT SORT OF REAL

Xmas 2017

Dear Sadhbh

Hope you enjoy this story. A little bit of history.

Love
Ada

MY STORY series

In chronological order:

SURVIVING SYDNEY COVE,
the Diary of Elizabeth Harvey,
Sydney, 1790
by Goldie Alexander

THE RUM REBELLION,
the Diary of David Bellamy,
Sydney Town, 1807–1808
by Libby Gleeson

A BANNER BOLD,
the Diary of Rosa Aarons,
Ballarat Goldfield, 1854
by Nadia Wheatley

THE YANKEE WHALER,
the Diary of Thomas Morris,
Bunbury WA, 1876
by Deborah Lisson

PLAGUES AND FEDERATION,
the Diary of Kitty Barnes,
The Rocks, Sydney, 1900
by Vashti Farrer

A DIFFERENT SORT OF REAL,
the Diary of Charlotte McKenzie,
Melbourne, 1918-1919
by Kerry Greenwood

WHO AM I?
the Diary of Mary Talence,
Sydney, 1937
by Anita Heiss

A TALE OF TWO FAMILIES,
the Diary of Jan Packard,
Melbourne, 1974
by Jenny Pausacker

MY STORY

A DIFFERENT SORT OF REAL

The Diary of
Charlotte McKenzie,
Melbourne 1918-1919

by Kerry Greenwood

A Scholastic Press book
from
Scholastic Australia

This book is for Jean Greenwood
who taught me to love history.

LEXILE™ 730

Scholastic Press
345 Pacific Highway
Lindfield NSW 2070
an imprint of Scholastic Australia Pty Limited (ABN 11 000 614 577)
PO Box 579, Gosford NSW 2250.
www.scholastic.com.au

Part of the Scholastic Group
Sydney ● Auckland ● New York ● Toronto ● London ● Mexico City
● New Delhi ● Hong Kong

First published in 2001.
Text copyright © Kerry Greenwood 2001.

Reprinted in 2002 (twice).

All rights reserved. No part of this publication may be reproduced or
transmitted in any form or by any means, electronic or mechanical, including
photocopying, recording, storage in an information retrieval system, or otherwise,
without the prior written permission of the publisher, unless specifically permitted
under the Australian Copyright Act 1968 as amended.

National Library of Australia Cataloguing-in-Publication entry
  Greenwood, Kerry.
  A different sort of real: the diary of Charlotte McKenzie, Melbourne 1918-1919.

  ISBN 1 86504 383 4.

  1. Influenza – Australia – Juvenile fiction. 2. Australia – Juvenile fiction.
  I. Title. (Series: My Story)
A823.3

Cover design by Antart, Sydney.

Typeset in Times.

Printed by McPherson's Printing Group, Maryborough Vic.

10 9 8 7 6 5 4 3   2 3 4 5 / 0

The Diary of

Charlotte McKenzie,

Melbourne 1918-1919

16th October 1918

Charlotte McKenzie is my name
Australia is my nation
Writing is my favourite game
And God is my salvation.

It's my birthday and I'm writing with my very best nib and Mum's Superfine ink in the blank book that Uncle Donald sent me from France. It is made of very beautiful paper and is bound in very elegant blue leather and I love it.

I asked Miss Tennant at school about writing a diary and she said that diaries are 'valuable historical records'. She also told me to 'write what I know' so I'll write about my family and myself in case someone in the future wants to know how we lived.

My name is Charlotte Isabelle McKenzie and I live in Seddon with my sister Amelia who is twelve, my other sister Lily who is ten, and the baby Albert who is six. My mother is a nurse and my father doesn't do anything since he came home from the war. He just complains about everything while Mum and I do all the work. Amelia helps but Lily is a lazybones and Albert is too little—besides, he's a boy.

The best thing that happened today was that Mum took me into the backyard and showed me my present. She opened the door to the shed next to the copper, which used to be full of broken furniture that Dad never got around to fixing, and there was my bed, my wardrobe, a table and chair and a washstand. The floor has a blue canvas covering and there are blue curtains with daisies. My own little room. No need to share with Lily and Amelia. I was so overcome that I couldn't say a word.

Mum said, 'Don't you like it?' All I could do was hug her. She laughed and said that a young lady needed her own room. She told me that my best friend Florence-next-door had chosen the colours.

Just then Florence and her big brother Alf came and brought me a blue bookcase. Alf was carrying it. It fitted beautifully across the back wall. They must have all been planning this for weeks and I never guessed. I had wondered why Mum had asked Mrs Quilty to come in and do the washing on a Wednesday, when I was at school, instead of on Saturday, when I was home to help. She didn't want me to open the shed door by mistake and spoil the surprise.

We all had cake and lemonade and they all sang happy birthday. Then Dad said that it was a waste of money and did we think he was made of pennies, which is unfair. Mum earns most of the money and she paid for it out of her own wages. But instead of arguing with him

Mum said that the material had cost next to nothing and the rest of the work had been done by Alf and his friends as a present and he needn't worry. Even that didn't please Dad but he stamped outside to smoke his pipe and left us in peace. He wasn't like this before he went away. I remember him when I was a child. He used to play games with me and carry me on his shoulders and he was almost never cross. Now he's cross all the time. Mum said it was the war and we mustn't mind. But I do mind.

Anyway then we all went for a walk to the Yarraville Gardens. We wore our best cotton dresses. Mine is dark blue with daisies. Florence's is bright yellow with spots. The little girls wore white muslin. Our hats are straw with matching bands. Florence and I sat near the aviary and talked and the children ran around. Mum got on with her mending. I gave Florence the latest war news. I can't talk about the war at home as Dad will not allow it. 'It looks as though it really will be over soon,' I told Florence.

I told Florence that the *Argus* thinks that it really will be over by Christmas this time. Mum said, 'Amen', and let the sock she was mending drop into her lap.

Florence's father is our local doctor, Dr Barnes. She said that he had told her that the armies have *la grippe*, a three day influenza, not dangerous but very exhausting. That won't help them win the war.

'We had a lot of cases through the Queen Victoria Hospital in the last few months,' said Mother. 'Charlotte caught it, remember? The rest of us were spared. Disease is not on anyone's side. We'll catch it the same as the enemy. The soldiers must be so tired and weak after so long in the mud; poor food, terrible hygiene, constant fear, no wonder they catch things.'

'Is that what happened to Dad?' I dared to ask.

'I don't know what happened to him,' said Mum. 'He's never said. He was gassed, I know that. I believe that he might have been buried when his trench collapsed. We have to be kind to him, Charlotte.'

I agreed.

Then we went home and had a birthday tea of fish cakes made of tinned salmon and baked potatoes. A great treat. Then I took my candle and went to bed in my own little room, very happy and thankful.

Now that I am writing this down, I imagine how it feels to have a ton of earth fall on you, to be buried, still breathing, earth in your mouth, earth in your ears, blinded, deaf, terrified. I am resolved to be kind to my father.

17th October

So much for good resolutions. This morning I was getting the children off to school as usual. I have to get them up, dress them, make their lunches, feed them breakfast and set them on their way. Then I have to clear the table, wash the dishes, sweep the floor, set the table for dinner and then run all the way to get to school in time. I was late because Lily is such a lazybones and wouldn't get up until I hauled her out of bed and smacked her. Then she grizzled. Amelia let the porridge scorch. The baker was late with the bread and the milk was on the turn.

The noise was upsetting Dad, I could see that. But I was in a hurry. I finally got everyone ready and shoved them out the door, then flew around setting everything to rights so it would be ready when Mum came home at nine. I rattled the dishes into the sink and slung the big kettle on the stove. Then I swept the floor. While I was doing this I accidentally knocked against the corner of the table and a cup rolled and smashed.

Dad yelled at me, 'Do you have to make so much noise, you clumsy girl? Can't you manage simple tasks without giving me a headache?'

I was doing my best. I picked up the pieces without a word and tiptoed out, got my hat and gloves and closed the front door very softly. I was seething with anger. He just sits there, not moving a finger, and he yells at me because I can't do all the work quietly enough for his taste. It's not fair. War or no war. It's not fair.

Later

I am writing this at the table.

Here is my family at tea. Dad sitting at the head of the table, carrying on about Albie using too much tomato sauce. Albie would be perfectly happy with tomato sauce and bread. Lily nibbling at half of her pie and then asking to get down and then sitting there and sulking because she wants to go and play with her doll. Amelia and I eating slowly because Mum says that if we just gobble she doesn't feel that all that work was worth it. Milk for all of us children, tea for Mum and Dad. Amelia is saying that her friend Muriel is having a birthday party and can she go? Dad forbids this because we can't afford to have a birthday party for Amelia in return. Amelia leaves the table in tears.

Mum says to Dad, 'Really, Alec.'

Dad says, 'The girl must learn how poor we are.'

Mum says, 'We know how poor we are, dear, but that doesn't mean we can't have any treats.'

Dad pushes back his chair and yells, 'I know it's all my fault,' and then stamps down the passage and slams the front door.

We know that he's gone to the pub, but it's such a relief that he's gone that we all sigh. Amelia comes back and Mum tells her that she can go to the party and not to tell Dad, lets Lily down so she can play with her doll, pours herself another cup of tea and tries to smile at us. 'It will be all right,' she says, but I don't believe her. Why can't I have a reasonable father like other girls?

It's a pity I don't like my father because I'm the only one in the family who looks like him. Lily and Amelia and even Albert are fair skinned and fair haired, like Mum, though she's getting grey hair now. I'm sallow with dark brown hair and Dad's brown eyes. They cut my hair when I had the flu and now it's growing out into curls. I'm pleased with the curls. I think I'll keep it short, even though Grandma McKenzie says that long hair is a woman's crowning glory. I don't need a crown.

Mum's made a pie tonight. Dad says they aren't as good as his mother's pies. He always says things like that.

Later still

Dad didn't come back until long after six o'clock, when the pubs closed. From my new beautiful room I heard him come in and I hastily blew out my candle. Mum lets me read until nine o'clock but when Dad is cranky he'll yell at anyone. Besides, until I get a clock or a watch I don't know what time it is.

I'm writing this by moonlight. It's very quiet in the yard, just birds rustling in the leaves of the lemon tree and a quiet mew from my black cat, Sable, telling me that he wants to come in and sleep on my bed. This is also forbidden but I leave the window open so he can get in. He's a very nice mannered cat—except he takes up a lot of the bed. I like being in my new room, outside the house. Our house is full of unhappiness.

18th October

Mum made me apologise to Dad for breaking the cup. I didn't want to but I did it. I don't think I was very convincing. Mum won't even suggest to him that he could do some of the work. Today is Friday and tomorrow we have to do the wash. I suppose I should describe that.

We haven't got a modern house so our copper is still heated by a fire. It lives in the same building as my new beautiful room, with a couple of cement washtroughs. I've already laid the fire, strung the washing lines and filled the copper so we can start early and with any luck get everything done by noon. I don't mind washing. It's hard work and the washing soda makes my hands sore, but it's out in the open and the weather is fine so it all ought to get dry. Mrs Quilty comes in to help with the washing. It's a three woman job for a family of six.

I want to read my new book. It's *A Little Bush Maid* by Mary Grant Bruce. I just had time to look at the first page, which looks really interesting, when I was called away to slice the bread for tea. Amelia is too young to be trusted with the bread knife.

We have our main meal at night, not like most other people who have dinner at noon, because our mother has to sleep during the day as she works all night at the hospital. The school doesn't mind if we girls stay and eat our sandwiches there while all the others go home. Florence keeps us company, and Lily's friend Muriel. Little Albie goes to Miss Templar's room with some other little children. It gives me time to sew. I'm making pillow cases at the moment. Mum does the mending and Amelia does the embroidery. She does beautiful drawn thread work. All I ever get out of drawn threads is knots, so I do the plain sewing. It's not difficult once you get used to it.

19th October

Mrs Quilty came very early and we had the first wash on the line by six o'clock. Another advantage of being outside is that I wake up when the sun rises. My window faces east. I lit the fire under the copper at five and the water was boiling and full of sheets by five-thirty. 'Good to get a jump on the day,' as Mrs Quilty says. She's a widow with five children so she works very hard. She's also very strong. It takes both me and Amelia, one on each end, to wring out a sheet over the copper stick, but Mrs Quilty can do it on her own.

Lily got up at seven and came out to feed the chooks, which is her job. By then we had most of the wash on the line, including Mum's uniforms and aprons which have to be soaked to remove the stains and then clear starched. Mrs Quilty is a wizard at clear starching. Lil was half asleep but she loves the chickens and they all flocked to her and pecked at the potato peelings and grain which she throws in little handfuls, to keep them with her as she calls them all by name. Specky, Spotty, Whitey, Red, Miss Jones and Mrs Chapman. Lil names her chooks after people she likes. She looked very pretty with her long hair over her shoulders and the chickens all around her. And she found six eggs, which is half a dozen. Lily is allowed to take her eggs to the grocer's and sell them. She buys chicken feed out of the money. Specky is broody, so soon we might have chicks.

Dad got up and went to the Repat Hospital for his appointment. The doctors don't do him any good, he says.

We had finished the wash, Mum was changing her clothes and we were sitting down for a cup of tea when Albie, who was sitting on the floor playing trains with a lot of empty cans, suddenly went blue. I grabbed him and he jerked. I prised his mouth open and saw something dark at the back of his throat. It was smooth and I couldn't get hold of it. Albie was getting bluer. I didn't know what to do.

Mrs Quilty grabbed him by the ankles and swung him into the air. Then she dealt him a hard blow in the middle and out popped the top of a medicine bottle.

'There you are, my lad,' said Mrs Quilty. She wasn't even worried. 'Someone's probably missing that bottle top,' she said calmly, putting Albie down on the floor and patting him on the head. Albie was so astonished he didn't even cry. I put the bottle top on the mantelpiece and when Mum came in she didn't notice. She had enough to worry her. And she'd told Amelia to look after Albert, who is always putting things into his mouth, ever since he was a baby. She's also told Dad not to leave his medicine bottles around. I didn't want to get Amelia into trouble. You have to watch Albie like a hawk and she was embroidering a present for Mum.

But I came over all dizzy and went to lie down. Just so quickly and easily our little brother could have been dead.

Later

I heard a whistle in the street as I was mixing the scone dough and then a rap at the door. Amelia opened it and there was a telegraph boy. She went white. Telegrams are expensive and are only sent in emergencies. Almost all of the women in my street had received a telegram from the War Office which said 'Your son has fallen, fighting gallantly in the service of his country'.

Mum said as she ran up the hall, 'Oh, my God, not Donald.'

Her brother Donald is in the Light Horse and she has always been worried about him. He's her favourite and only brother and she says he's too bold. She gave the boy a penny and ripped open the telegram while I stood there up to my wrists in flour.

Then Mum came in smiling. 'Dad has to stay in hospital for a few days for some tests on his heart,' she said. 'I'll have to send you and Amelia with his night things. I'll pack them up directly.'

Dad away? It would be like a holiday. I finished the scones. Amelia and I took the bag and went off to catch the train at Yarraville Station. I love catching trains. It's an adventure. I love the chuff, the steam, the sense of moving as fast as a bird flying. I was wearing my school gloves so that I could put the return half of our tickets in the left-hand palm so we shouldn't lose them.

We got out at Flinders Street Station and caught a tram to the Repatriation Hospital. I like trams too. At the hospital we handed over the bag to the lady at the desk. She was just asking us how old we were when a man screamed, a terrible noise, and then came running into the cool foyer, holding his head and making this terrible noise. He fell to his knees and a couple of orderlies tackled him and hauled him away. He was screaming words now. 'Shelling, shelling, it's in my head, it's in my head. Get down! Put out that light! They're sending over hell and damnation. Get down!'

Amelia and I edged closer to the reception nurse. She gave us a swift pat. 'It's all right, girls, he won't hurt you, poor fellow.'

'What's wrong with him?' I asked.

'Shell shock, like your father,' she said absent mindedly. 'Tell your mother that he'll be home in a few days, and take care on the train. Have you got your tickets?'

I showed her the return halves and she gave us a penny each for an ice-cream and told us we were brave girls.

Shell shock? What is shell shock? I am writing this in my own little room, waiting for Florence next door to smuggle out her father's textbook which mentions shell shock. Another advantage of my room is that I can talk to Florence through the fence without anyone overhearing us.

Amelia didn't seem to notice the fact that the nurse had told us Dad's secret. She just told me that strawberry was her favourite ice-cream and I already knew that. We bought a ha'penny ice each and saved a whole penny. We ate them while walking through the park.

20th October

The Vicar gave a nice sermon on the possibility of peace and the value of charity, which I think I've heard before.

Lily is perfectly good in church now we've moved to a pew where she can see her face in a brass plate on the wall. Lily finds her reflection very interesting. I'm sure she's vain. I'm not, but I haven't anything to be vain about. I'm not the one with the long golden curls.

Sunday lunch was an egg and bacon pie instead of the roast that Dad says we must have, and we were all very happy. Mum brought out the Sunday books and Amelia and I played spillikins. She always wins because her hands are steadier than mine. Mum even sang us some songs. She used to sing a lot until Dad said she was off-key and made his head hurt. I like 'Cherry Ripe', Amelia likes 'The Yeomen of England' and Lily loves 'Lily of Laguna'—vain thing—and 'There's a Long Long Trail' because it's so sad. It was so sad and Mum sang it so beautifully that we all burst into tears and then laughed at ourselves and made tea. Mum let me have some, in a china cup with rosebuds on. I felt like a real lady.

22nd October

Florence snuck her father's textbook to me through the fence last evening but I didn't have time to look at the because after I'd talked to Florence for a while, her father came to the door and called her in. Suddenly I was so tired that I just washed my face and hands and put myself to bed. Then this morning I had to get ready for school. I hoped that Florence's father hadn't noticed that his *Principles of Neuropathology* was missing. I could have asked him, perhaps, but he's such a bear of a man and he would never lend me the book without wanting to know why I wanted it and I can't tell him. I'm sure that Dad would never want anyone to know he had shell shock. I've never heard of it. No one talks about it.

Later

I can't understand this book. It's got too many long words in it. It talks about 'neurasthenia' and 'hypochondria' and 'depression' and all I've managed to find out is that shell shock happens to soldiers who were in the front line for too long, that it has something to do with sensitivity to noise and nothing to do with cowardice. It even affects horses and dogs. But in humans it is very bad. It makes them nervous and sick and full of nightmares. Sometimes it makes them shake and sometimes it makes them mad like the man in the hospital, or deaf, or mute, or blind. They get heart attacks and asthma and something called 'night sweats' and 'soldier's heart'. And if I've read this bit right it says that they sometimes, no, surely not, it says here that sometimes they kill themselves.

And there's no cure. I wish I hadn't tried to find out. Grandma McKenzie always told me that curiosity killed the cat.

I'll give the book back tomorrow, before school.

23rd October

Wednesday. The most awful thing happened, I sneaked through the gap in the fence to give Florence her book back and Doctor Barnes caught me. He's big and old and has a black beard and I've always been scared to death of him. He barked at me, 'Who's there?' and when I said it was me he said, 'And what brings you to the back door, young lady?'

I was fairly caught then because he saw the book and knew it was his. So I held it out and said, 'I was returning this book, Sir,' and I was about to apologise because Florence had pinched it without asking when he looked puzzled and said, 'Why on earth did you want

Principles of Neuropathology? Were you pressing flowers?'

Then I was quite offended because men always assume that girls can't think about anything but knitting patterns and new hats and babies so I told him I wanted to consult it about shell shock. He made me come inside and sit down at the kitchen table with Mrs Reilly, his cook. She gave me a cup of tea and a currant scone warm from the oven.

'So you wanted to know about shell shock?' he said, quite kindly, but still with that half smile which means that at any moment he was about to say, 'There, there, little girl, go away and play with your doll.'

'Yes,' I said.

'And how did you get on with neuropathology?' he asked.

'I understood about depression,' I told him. 'But I didn't know some of the words. What's neurasthenia? Is it the same as nervous exhaustion?'

He was looking a little surprised.

'Of course, her mother is a nurse. That's where she has picked up these terms, and she's parroting them,' he said indulgently to the cook.

'No, I haven't spoken to my mother about this,' I insisted. What is wrong with men? Do you have to be male to be considered sane?

I couldn't stand being condescended to any more, so

I stood up to go and thanked him for the loan of his book, Then—because I was very cross—I said, 'If I was a boy, would you think I was parroting?'

The cook coughed. Dr Barnes scowled. Then he reached out a hand and touched my arm.

'I beg your pardon,' he said, seeming to mean it. 'Do sit down. You are correct. If you were a boy, I would consider you a promising pupil. These days, when women mine coal and drive trains and practise in my profession, I cannot afford to make the old pre-war assumptions. Dear me, no. Well. Shell shock. No one quite knows the cause, and no one has a cure which will work in all cases. The advice I always give to the relatives of the afflicted is that what the person most needs is to feel needed. Visible wounds elicit sympathy. Invisible ones merely make the sufferer feel inadequate. They are always tired, headachy, sensitive to noise, touchy and erratic. But your father still loves you, you know,' he added.

'Thank you,' I said, turning my head in case I started to cry.

He let me out the back door and told me that if I liked I could borrow any of his books and I climbed back through the fence. It was time to get the children up and off to school. All the time I was making the porridge and pouring the milk I was considering what I hadn't said to Dr Barnes. The question was not if my father still loved me. It was whether I still loved him, or what he had become..

That's such a terrible thing to write that I will stop now, go back into the house, and listen to my mother singing 'Lily of Laguna.'

24th October

We have been so busy today. Mrs Barnes brought a lot of wool home from the Ladies' Auxiliary at the hospital and it all has to be wound from skeins into balls for the ladies who knit socks for soldiers. Florence and I dragged Alf and Amelia into this task and it was fun, because Dr Barnes has a phonograph and seven records and we were allowed to play them while we were winding. One of the songs is about a nurse. It's called 'The Rose of No Man's Land'. When Mum came to get us we played it to her and she blushed. I haven't seen Mum blush for such a long time.

Dr Barnes invited Mum to take a glass of sherry and she accepted and sat down while Florence and I finished packing the balls of wool into boxes. 'Seventeen cases this week,' I heard Mum say to the doctor.

He shook his head. 'I don't like it. Flu this late in the year. Well, it's in God's hands, as usual. Fine intelligent daughter you have, Mrs McKenzie,' he said to Mum, looking at me. 'Good brain.'

Then I blushed. We were doing a lot of blushing, us McKenzies.

'My Charlotte?' said Mum. 'Well, yes, she's always been clever.'

'Is she leaving school next year?' he asked.

'Yes,' said Mum. 'She can't be a nurse until she is eighteen so we'll have to find her another job in between.'

'Seems a pity,' said Dr Barnes. I didn't hear the rest, for we were loading Alf up with the boxes to take outside to the pony cart for Mrs Barnes to deliver the next day. I wonder what that was all about?

28th October

Monday again and Dad's back and worse than ever. He's stopped yelling at us. He's stopped talking, too. He just sits there, staring out of the window. Or into the fire. He seems to be always cold so Mum makes me light the fire before I leave and she tends it during the day.

I came home from school pleased that I had got ten out of ten for a mathematics test. Mum had gone to fetch Albie from the yard and Dad was just sitting, staring into the ashes. He hadn't even been able to put the coal on.

It's awful. There doesn't seem to be anything I can do. Mum says I mustn't call in Dr Barnes because he might send Dad off to the Insane Asylum and then we'd never get him back. But it's like living with a ghost. He'll eat if someone brings him a plate and sometimes he'll notice us. He noticed Albie when he fell over the coal scuttle and hurt his hand. I heard the clatter and ran into the parlour to fetch him and found him sitting on Dad's knee. Dad's arm was around him and he was leaning down to kiss his hand better. Albie stopped crying right away. But Dad didn't say anything and his eyes got this glazed look and he didn't stop Albie when he got down.

We're collecting pennies for our guy. It's bonfire night next week. I've already got eightpence ha'penny for crackers.

5th November

Tuesday and it's bonfire night. We've built a big fire up on the paddock, away from any overhanging trees, and the boys have been bringing in all sorts of things: broken chairs, old mattresses, logs. We've got potatoes to roast and ninepence three farthings of crackers and we're all going, even Albie, though Mum made me promise to bring him home before eleven o'clock or if he got sleepy or frightened. Florence's mother gave us an old straw hat for our guy and he's got overalls and a pitchfork. I've taught Albie the rhyme:

> *Remember, remember the fifth of November*
> *Gunpowder treason and plot.*
> *I see no reason why gunpowder treason*
> *Should ever be forgot.*

Except he keeps saying 'pleason and trot', he's learned it very well. He's such a clever little boy.

Lily insists on having her hair plaited and wearing a bonnet in case of soot and Amelia always squeaks at every bang, but it should be fun.

Later

We had a lovely time at the bonfire. Our guy burned beautifully and we all got sooty from roast potatoes, even Lily. They taste so much better than ordinary potatoes even though they are black on the outside and not very well cooked or burned to charcoal. It's fine to be out in the street in the dark. Albie didn't say a word, bless him. We came home with Florence and we were laughing when we came inside and heard this strange noise.

When we got into the parlour, there was Dad on the floor. His face was purple. He was in a fit. I told the others to try to hold him still and ran for Dr Barnes. He came with me right away, in his pyjamas and topcoat and I carried his bag.

Then he sent the others into the kitchen and told me to hold my father's arms while he shoved a pencil between his back teeth. Then he barked 'Blankets!' at me and I dragged the blankets off Mum's bed and we wrapped him. Then Dr Barnes snapped 'Bag!' and I brought the bag. He took out a bottle and dripped brandy through those drawn-back lips.

'Is he going to . . . ?' I asked, still holding Dad as tight as I could.

'No,' he said shortly. 'This is the fifth I've seen tonight. It's the crackers. The bangs. Last time he heard noises like that, they were high explosive shells and someone was about to be killed. There. It's all right, old fellow,' he said to Dad. 'We'll get you to bed now. Help me, Charlotte,' he said, and I went into the bedroom and pulled off Dad's slippers while Dr Barnes wrestled him out of his coat and trousers. 'We'll lift him at three,' he told me. 'One, two, three,' and it wasn't that hard to lift Dad. I tucked him into bed and Dr Barnes got some more brandy into his mouth and he swallowed.

Then Dr Barnes beckoned to me and, taking a medicine bottle, we went out and half closed the door.

'Has this happened before?' he asked me, sternly.

'No,' I said.

'This is why you wanted to know about shell shock,' he stated.

'Yes,' I said.

'How long has he been taking paraldehyde?' he asked. I recognised the bottle. The Repat had sent him home with it.

'Two weeks,' I said. I knew because the stuff had a peculiar, very nasty smell, like phenol and old drains.

'And he's taken all this in two weeks?'

'I suppose so,' I replied. The pint bottle was nearly empty.

Dr Barnes said a very rude word.

'Who's his doctor?' he asked.

'The hospital ones,' I said.

Dr Barnes damned and blasted all hospitals.

'I'll come by in the morning. Charlotte, you did very well. Now, you'd better calm the children; they will have got a fright. You too, of course,' he added, and patted me, not on the head as though I was a child, but on the shoulder as though I was a lady.

'Doctor,' I said. I didn't want to say this but I had to.

'Miss McKenzie?'

'We can't afford . . .'

He wouldn't let me finish the sentence. He said something like 'Humph!' and let himself out.

I told the children that Dad was all right and made some hot milk and we sat in the kitchen sipping it and telling stories until Albie fell asleep and Lily and Amelia washed their faces and hands and went to bed.

I went and sat by Dad's bed until I was sure he was asleep. Then I came back here to write it all down. It's very dark and late and Mrs Quilty is coming to do the washing tomorrow, no, today, because she is going to a wedding on Saturday and I have to stay home from school to help. And I don't know what Mum is going to say, but I don't see what else I could have done.

6th November

Mum was about to be cross with me when she came home but Dr Barnes arrived just as she was noticing the mess in the parlour. He explained it all to her and told her that Dad was poisoning himself with paraldehyde. He said it was lucky that I had called him because now Dad would be under his care. He could promise that he would regain some of his wits as long as she hid the bottle and only gave him the right dose. He also said that he would require no payment until I had finished school for the summer when he wished to employ me to help him in his Dispensary for Poor People, which he holds once a week.

'If one cannot get a qualified person, I cannot think of anyone better than a neat handed young woman with no fiddle-faddles and a prompt intelligent mind,' he said, scowling at me.

I am not sure what a fiddle-faddle is but I am pleased that I don't have any. Mum was a little taken aback but she agreed and we went to tackle the washing. I was delighted. This would be excellent training for when I am a nurse.

The trouble with housework is that it never stops and no one ever notices it unless it is not done. Mrs Quilty grumbled a bit at the soot on the pillow cases but it came out in the wash.

The newspaper which Florence showed me said that President Wilson's Fourteen Points were the basis of an Armistice Proposal to be offered to Germany now that they have got rid of the Kaiser. Horrible old man. I could never love a man with moustaches like that. Florence says that even a buck's horn moustache may cover a gentle heart but I don't believe it. In any case, it can't. It's in the wrong place.

10th November. Sunday

It was raining hard so Mum said that we didn't have to go to church but instead we could read a chapter of the Bible each. It was Lily's choice and she chose Job. I can't imagine why she likes Job. The same reason why she likes sad songs, I suppose. We read through God striking Job with blains and boils and the poor man sitting on a heap of stones while everyone told him that his misfortunes must have been his own fault because no one loses all their wives and camels and sons and concubines and wealth and gets blains without having deserved it. Which isn't true. Job was perfectly innocent and I think it was very unkind and unfair of God to smite him like that just to win a bet with Satan. And when in the end he gives Job back his camels and things, Job is supposed to be happy that he was tested. I don't approve. And I must borrow the big dictionary from Florence and find out what 'blains' are. They sound worse than boils.

Dad seems better, more awake. When I said something about how Job hadn't deserved to be blighted, he said in a rusty, creaky voice, 'Sometimes evil things just happen, daughter, and one must bear with them.'

Then we had a proper dinner in the middle of the day, like everyone else has. Mum had bought a leg of mutton. Dad ate quite a lot and didn't even yell at us when Lily slapped Amelia for cheating at Snap. He just took the cards away and told us we were godless heathens, almost like he used to.

I almost think that things might be getting better.

12th November

We were at school and reading Shakespeare and I had just got to Othello's lament, 'Farewell pomp and circumstance of glorious war ! Othello's occupation gone!', when there was a noise of many voices outside. First Miss Tempest said, 'Girls, please, resume your seats,' but she went to the window and soon we could all hear boys yelling and women screaming out, 'It's over!' Then poor Miss Tempest couldn't stop us running out of the classroom and into the yard.

I ran out into the street because people were dancing. They were really dancing, and laughing. I have never heard such a noise before. I snatched a newspaper as it went past and Florence leaned over my shoulder to read it. A tress of her red hair tickled my nose. Florence's hair always comes unplaited in moments of excitement. The paper said: 'Armistice Signed Guns Fall Silent On The Western Front' and that at the eleventh hour of the eleventh day of the eleventh month of nineteen eighteen the War was over, the Great War, the War to End War.

It was no use asking us to be Proper Young Ladies, we tore off our hats and cheered.

The Colonial Sugar dray went past and one of the girls knew Florence and held out her hands and helped us up onto the dray. We were in the middle of a cheering, dancing, weeping crowd. The four big horses clipped along; the girls and men were a much lighter load than tons of sugar. The wind blew our hair back and we started to laugh and couldn't stop. 'It's over! It's over!' Everyone was yelling. In the crowd there were women in black who were weeping as though their hearts were broken for their sons and brothers and husbands who would never come home even if the war was over. I was suddenly so sorry for them that I started to cry as well and Doreen, Florence's friend (she used to work in Florence's house as a maid until she decided she'd rather work in a factory), kissed me and told me it was all over and now the boys would be coming home and there'd be plenty for me as long as I didn't want her Billy. That was such a silly thing to say that I stopped crying and Florence lent me her handkerchief.

We rode along, above the crowd like queens, caught up in the pure joy. No one was drunk. No one was angry. Everyone was just happy, terribly, terribly happy.

Florence and I slipped off the dray as it passed the Town Hall. We let the crowd go and then ran back to school as fast as we could, adding up our sins. Leaving the classroom without permission. Leaving the school yard without permission.

'Worst of all,' said Florence as she puffed beside me, 'being seen in public without our hats or gloves. And running.'

'This is not the conduct of a Proper Young Lady,' I told her as we rounded the corner and slipped through the back gate. It is supposed to be kept locked but it usually isn't because it's too much trouble to be constantly locking and unlocking it whenever a cart wants to come in, and the gate keeper is very old. He was in the Crimea. He saw Florence Nightingale. Or so he says.

He came rumbling out of his cottage and snarled, 'What are you doing here?'

We said, 'The War's over, Bill!' He didn't believe us until Florence showed him our newspaper. Then he came over funny and went back into his cottage without a word.

Florence and I sneaked back to our classroom and found it empty. Then we heard singing and crept to the hall. The whole school was in a service of thanksgiving. We slipped in through the back as they got to the second verse of 'Oh God Our Help In Ages Past'.

'Beneath the shadow of thy throne,' I sang as I moved through the ranks, slotting into place next to Mary Johnson.

'Thy saints have dwelt secure.' Florence was beside me.

Miss Tempest gave us a sharp look, shook her head, and then nodded. We breathed a sigh of relief into the third verse and smuggled her our newspaper. One good turn deserves another. I saw her fold it and lay it across her open hymn book. Miss Tempest's young man was in the army. I saw her begin to smile.

'The Great War is over,' announced Miss Green. 'The Armistice is signed. This is a day of heartfelt rejoicing and I am declaring a half holiday for the entire school.'

We all cheered and those of us who had hats flung them into the air.

I found Lily and Amelia and collected Albie from Infants' and we all walked home. People were riding past on bicycles or racing past on foot, crying, 'It's over, it's over at last!'

No more telegrams telling of sudden death and loss. No more war news to keep from Dad. No more khaki cloth and no more socks to knit, bandages to roll, pennies to save, no more war.

I felt very happy but also a little wobbly. There had been a war for so long. Since I was ten. Now there was no more war, what would happen to all those men, and how would we fit them into their families again? There's more to tell, but I can't write any more tonight.

13 November

After we got back yesterday, Florence made us go into her house to have lemonade and cakes. Mrs Reilly was crying for joy and making biscuits. She allowed Albie to lick the bowl. He got Anzac mixture all over him. Albie loves treacle. He's the stickiest child in the world. He even got treacle in his hair but Mrs Reilly was so happy that she offered to wash him in hot water from the gas-boiler. I had never seen one of these before. You just turn the tap and hot water pours out. Such a convenience. We lathered Albie in the sink and rough dried him. He was clean and very pleased because by then the Anzac biscuits had come out of the oven and he adores Anzacs.

'Now the boys will come home,' said Mrs Reilly. She has three sons in the navy and she prays for them every night, Florence says.

'Give the child another biscuit, God love him,' Mrs Reilly said.

Lily, who loves dainty things, had a sugared cake with a crystallised violet on top. Florence and I ate a lot of everything.

'Florence,' I said, 'can the others stay here while I go in and tell Dad? He might not be quite pleased.' Florence understood at once and I left the feast and went next door.

The house was dark. I went into the parlour and there was Dad, staring into the fire, though it was bright sunshine outside.

'Dad?' I asked.

'What is it,' he said. At least he wasn't yelling.

'The war's over, Dad,' I said.

'It's never over,' he said, still in that flat voice. 'It'll never be over. Listen to the fools laughing,' he said. So he had heard the crowd, even inside with the door shut fast.

'We're next door,' I said hurriedly. 'We've got a half holiday and we didn't want to wake you.'

'Wake me? I wish you could.' He stared at me for a moment then looked away. 'Your mother's gone with the crowd, too. Go on, Charlotte. Have fun. But don't expect me to join in.'

'No, Dad,' I said, and ran back to Florence's house.

We stayed for high tea. It was wonderful. There was ham and fried eggs and kedgeree and sardines and scones and cakes and sandwiches. Florence and I had tea, like ladies, and even Amelia tried it, but made a face and said she liked milk better. Albie ate more than any child could possibly hold and then went to sleep listening to the phonograph.

Lily played 'There's a Long Long Trail a-Winding' six times until Mrs Barnes begged for mercy. We all agreed that it had been the nicest day of our lives.

When Mum came to fetch us she seemed younger. Her hair was coming out of its bun. We thanked Mrs Barnes for our tea and walked out into the dark.

'You're all very good children,' said Mum. 'The war's over and now, please God, Donnie will be coming home.'

15th November

School is all exams and I have been studying as much as I can while doing all my tasks. I think I should be all right in English and I always get top marks in mathematics, history and science but I'm not too sure of geography and Latin. I'll need Latin if I want to be a nurse because a lot of medicines and instructions are in Latin. I'll only need geography if I get lost on the Orinoco but I suppose this could happen.

18th November

I've done all my exams and now I can finally read the rest of *A Little Bush Maid*. I've been saving it up as a reward for finishing school. I ought to get my Intermediate Certificate all right if I didn't mess up the subjunctive in my Latin paper. Subjunctives are wriggly. I don't want to leave school, but we can't afford the fees to send me to a private school to do the last two years, Leaving and Matriculation, which I would need to get into university. Then we couldn't afford the fees for medical school so I'm only telling you this, diary, that I want to be a doctor. I'm going to settle for being a nurse. I'm clever enough to get through school, I think. But even if I saved for years I couldn't pay the university fees. It will have to wait until I am twenty-one. No one gives scholarships to girls.

It's unfair, but even Job got blains and he was more innocent than me. The world seems rather flat now that the war is over. Dad isn't any better but he's not any worse either. The weather's getting hotter. Soon we'll be able to take the children to the beach. Amelia, who is clever with her needle, is trimming our sun hats with very pretty rosebuds made of Mrs Barnes's silk scraps. Mrs Barnes likes pink. It's a pity that I don't because we've got a lot of pink.

Lily is pleased because her hen, Specky, has hatched out five chicks. Sable, the cat, is very interested in them but he knows better than to touch the chooks. I'll write some more when something happens.

11th December

I'm starting at Dr Barnes' Dispensary tomorrow. Mum has cut down two of her old aprons for me and I'm hemming them in my little room by the light of my candle. I asked her if she had any advice and she said, 'First, do exactly as the doctor tells you; second, if you don't understand what he wants, ask before you do anything; and third, never show a patient that you are shocked or disgusted.' I don't know how hard that will be. I'm practising keeping my face still.

Miss Tempest says that I did very well on the exam papers and she is very pleased with me. I even got an A for Latin so I must have got that subjunctive right. Miss Tempest gave me a book, *Stories from the Lives of Noble Women*, and a silk bookmark. Janey signed my autograph book with 'When this you see remember me' and we were all very affected because it's not likely we will see each other again.

I got my Intermediate Certificate, which is very pretty with engraved edges. The school had an afternoon tea for us with cakes with pink icing and silver balls and I walked home with Florence. At least I'll see Florence again. She's going to Presbyterian Ladies' College next year. She'll never have to work and she isn't really interested in school, while I would love to go to school. The ways of the world are very odd because I'll have to find a job in a shop or something and Florence would love to work in a shop. She's interested in clothes, and I'm not. But, of course, Dr Barnes would never allow his daughter to work. And because of Dad, I have to. It's not that I mind working. It's just that—never mind.

Mum and I have chosen some good, hard-wearing printed calico for three dresses for me now that I don't have to wear that rotten box-pleated tunic any more. Or the round hat, felt for winter and straw for summer. Or those awful gloves. And I don't have to be a proper young lady any more. Which is a relief. Mum has cut out the dresses and I am sewing them as fast as I can. The first one will be finished in time to wear it tomorrow.

13th December

I went to be the doctor's assistant last night. His hours are from six to eight in the evening every Thursday. There is a separate entrance to his surgery and I went in in my apron. He grunted 'Good' at me and told me to tie a cloth around my head. Mrs Reilly gave me a white linen square. I felt like a real nurse.

There was a lot of people there. The first thing I noticed was the smell. They smelled of unwashed clothes and unwashed bodies and there was a strong smell of tar from Mr West who works on the road. He had a crushed finger. Doctor bade me soak the bandage off and clean the wound and then he'd have a look at it. I laid Mr West's hand in a dish and poured carbolic and water over it and he kept talking to me.

'Am I your first patient, then, girlie?' he said, very kindly. I started to peel off the filthy bandage and he said, 'Keep on, there, girlie, that's bonzer'. Then when I got the bandage off I could see bone, and his fingernail was hanging by a thread. I cleaned as much as I could and then Doctor came and said, 'Well, Mr West, that fingernail's gone but we might be able to save the finger.' He snipped off the nail and then stitched the tendons together and then the flesh. It looked like an awful mess to me. Mr West never moved.

Doctor said, 'Iodoform solution and then bandage him up, Miss McKenzie.'

I mixed the solution as it said on the bottle, then I thought I'd better ask, so I did, and instead of being angry he said, 'Quite right. I should have told you, double strength, four to one. I'm not used to having an assistant'.

So Mum was right, always ask. I did a nice bandage for Mr West, just like I learned in First Aid at school.

Then we had a lady who was expecting and had swollen ankles, and a boy with a cut across his head. Doctor told me to shave his head with a straight razor. I'd never used one and the boy kept fidgeting and whimpering and he smelled so bad that I had to keep holding my breath. That shaving soap was the first soap he'd seen in months. When I finally got the wound clean there were little red rings all over his scalp.

'Ringworm,' said Doctor. 'Wash out the wound with carbolic and then put iodine on each one of those sores. Miss McKenzie, you need to talk to your patients.

They're afraid. If you tell them what you are doing, they'll sit still.'

I said to the boy that I would have to wash out the cut on his head but he'd be all right if he just sat still and soon it would stop hurting. He smiled at me, poor little grimy boy. Doctor stitched him up and I dotted iodine on the ringworm and he howled because it stung. But he really liked his clean new bandage. Then I washed my hands in carbolic. The boy had head lice, of course. I cleaned up while Doctor talked to the lady with the swollen ankles. He was telling her to keep off her feet; she was telling him that she worked in a factory to feed her children and her invalid husband and how did he expect her to keep off her feet?

He gave her a bottle of the bright red tonic and she went away. Doctor Barnes said, 'Mothers!' and called in the next patient.

I'm so tired. I'll write more tomorrow.

These are called 'case notes' and all nurses keep them.

14th December

The next patient was a man with a high fever and chills. Doctor told him to go home, go to bed and drink lots of fluids and gave him a note for the boss and a bottle of brown medicine.

Then Doctor handed me a baby so wrapped up in blankets that it could not be seen and told me to bathe him in cool water. I've bathed Albie lots of times but this one was very hot. His mother was telling the doctor that little Billy wouldn't eat and vomited up his milk. I got Billy's nappy off and his bottom was raw, poor little thing. I bathed him and he threw up all over me, so I had to go and empty the baby bath and start again. Doctor asked what the mother had been giving Billy and she showed him a bottle of Dalby's Soothing Syrup. Dr Barnes seemed to grow into a giant and bellowed that she was poisoning the infant. She started to cry and said Billy screamed all the time and her husband was unable to sleep. Doctor pulled back her collar and there were bruises on her shoulder and on her wrists. Her husband must have been hitting her because the baby was crying.

'You mustn't give the baby any more of this stuff,' he said in a kinder voice. 'Billy cries because he is in pain. Here is some zinc and castor oil ointment for the nappy rash and he will start eating again when he feels comfortable. Miss McKenzie will show you how to mix it. Two oil to one zinc, Miss McKenzie.'

I dried the baby and mixed the ointment and when I smeared it on the poor mite he stopped crying at once. I gave him a clean nappy and the mother wrapped him again.

'One wrapping,' said the doctor. 'You'll overlay the poor child. Goodbye, Billy,' he said, shaking the baby's hand. When she was gone, he said 'Mothers!' again, in quite a different tone.

Then in came Mrs Thomas to have her varicose ulcers dressed. They were horrible, oozing and yellow, and the skin on her shins was as thin as paper. She kept apologising. I felt ashamed of my disgust. It wasn't poor Mrs Thomas's fault that she had ulcers. I cleaned and dried the ulcers and dressed them and bandaged them.

Then it was a little girl, Jane Markham, with a burned hand. Doctor gave her an injection of morphine. He says that burns hurt worse than any other injury, even a broken bone. Her father had held her palm on the flat iron because she was cheeky. Doctor told her mother she ought to go to the police. She said she couldn't because if they locked him up, who would feed the children? Doctor grunted. We use a smelly yellow ointment on burns and it stops the pain by sealing off the air. I gave Jane a sling and she stopped crying. Doctor told her to come back next week and maybe she might be able to use her hand again. It was her right hand.

Then we had several people with 'chests' who all went away with the bottle of the dark brown medicine which smelled like a freshly tarred road or a gas escape. One 'chest' worried the doctor. It was a young woman, Miss Jamieson, who was excited because she was about to be married. The doctor sent her to the hospital for an X-ray. While he was writing the note she told me about her wedding dress and the flowers she was going to have. 'White roses,' she said.

When she was gone the doctor rubbed his beard with both hands. He looked sad. I asked him why.

'I think she has TB,' he said. 'The white roses will come in handy to decorate her coffin, poor girl, not her wedding.'

I was shocked, but Mum had said never to look shocked, so I just nodded and went on with rolling up the unused bandages.

The clock struck. I was amazed that it was so late.

'It's eight,' said the doctor. 'No more patients. Shut up shop, Miss McKenzie. You did quite well,' he added. 'You're neat handed, you can obey orders, you ask if you don't know and you're not squeamish.' Then he added gently, 'And you are allowed to be affected by the tragedy of human life and death.'

I burst into tears. Poor Miss Jamieson! She was so happy about her wedding plans. Doctor Barnes patted me and sent me into the kitchen for a cup of tea and a biscuit. Mrs Reilly mopped me, put my cap and apron in a bucket of carbolic, and told me I was a brave girl, so I was.

And when I stopped crying I was so hungry that she made me a cheese sandwich.

If this is what being a doctor's assistant is like, I am

going to like it. But I did go home, heat water on the stove, and wash my hair in case I had caught nits from that filthy boy. Dad grumbled but Mum smiled at me. 'I did just the same after my first day, Charlotte,' she said. 'Don't go to bed until your hair is quite dry, now, or you'll catch cold.'

So this is the grown-up world. Fathers hurt their children, husbands hurt their wives and women hurt their babies, and all work and suffer. But then Mr West was terribly brave and Mrs Thomas as well. Even the filthy boy was brave enough once I told him what I was doing.

Now that I am at home, I have taken over the housekeeping. I need to do the grocery list. We're almost out of oatmeal.

Later

I made out the grocery list and went to Dad for the money. The grocer's boy comes by every Saturday for orders. We needed oatmeal, sandsoap, potatoes, salt, a pound of butter (at a shilling) and a pound of tea (at eleven pence, Best Blend, which is Dad's favourite). I hoped I might get some broken biscuits at tuppence the pound. Dad reached into his dressing-gown pocket and counted out the coins, complaining that everything cost a fortune. I had to stand there and listen to him because I had to have the money. He went on and on about having so many mouths to feed.

He seemed crouched and mean. I disliked him. Finally he counted out the money into my hand and I could run outside and give the list and the money to Jimmy, the grocer's boy. He winked at me and cycled off, whistling.

I wish I could cycle off. Dr Barnes came in before lunch and ordered me into the yard to put a chair under the lemon tree. We've got a big, old lemon tree and it is in flower and fruit. I had managed to mend a couple of the old chairs which used to be in my room and I put one next to the trunk. Then Dr Barnes came out, pushing Dad along in front of him like a hen with a chick, or a big sheepdog and a small sheep. He put Dad in the chair, wrapped a blanket around him, told me to fetch a cup of tea and my father's pipe, and gave Dad a newspaper.

'Time you got interested in something besides yourself, my lad,' he told Dad. 'You'll sit out here, not crouch in front of that fire, now the weather's turned warm. You can talk to the chooks. Always very soothing company, chooks.'

The funny thing was that Dad did as Dr Barnes said. He sat outside all day, sometimes reading but mostly watching Sable stalking through the tree and Specky tending her chicks. And he didn't yell once. I even took his lunch outside and set it up on another chair. It was only sandwiches but he ate three. I got the parlour cleaned, dusted, the grate emptied and the fire re-laid and the floor swept very quickly. It was much easier without

Dad stooped over the fire, brooding and getting cross if I asked him to move his feet. I even had time to finish my second dress. I sat outside with Dad, where the light is better. At first I did not know if he would send me away but he seemed pleased. Mrs Barnes had done the seams on her machine so I didn't have a lot to do, only the hems and the collars and cuffs. Dad even said, 'You sew well, Charlotte. Is this a new dress?' I told him about printed calico being very long wearing and he actually smiled and said, 'As long as it's pretty. Girls should have pretty dresses.'

Then he went to sleep and I tiptoed off to lay the table for dinner. Imagine! Dad saying anything nice!

16th December

Monday again. Dad's mood didn't last.

We were all talking about Christmas and Albie said he wanted chicken for Christmas dinner. Dad said that Lily should choose which chook he should kill. Lily burst into tears and said none of them. Mum said that Albie could go without chicken. Dad said that we were sentimental women and he'd kill one of the chickens for us. Lily screamed and Albie started to cry. I told Dad that all of Lily's chickens were laying and should not be eaten.

Dad said well if that's what we wanted and grabbed his coat and went out into the street.

I don't know what would have happened if he'd gone into the yard because by then Lily had screamed herself into hysterics. We only managed to calm her by telling her that I would watch her chickens and make sure that Dad didn't kill them and I had to promise. I'm sure that Dad didn't understand how fond Lily is of her chickens.

And it doesn't look like there will be much for Christmas. Amelia has embroidered things for everyone and I've bought a handkerchief each for Mum and Dad and made a toy train for Albie and strung beads for the girls. Pearl beads for Lily and scarlet ones for Amelia. It wouldn't matter that we were poor if we were happy. But we're not.

17th December

The strangest thing happened today. I was just bringing in the billy of milk before Sable got at it—he's found out how to knock off the lid, the clever puss—when I saw a man striding down the street as though he owned the world. He was in a soldier's uniform with emu feathers in his slouch hat, which made him a Light Horseman. He was carrying a big heavy swag as though it weighed no more than a bubble. I wondered who he was. He was so tall and healthy. All the men around here are sickly, crippled, very old or very young.

Then he turned in at our gate and grinned at me. His teeth were as white as seeds. His blue eyes twinkled.

'It's never little Charlotte, is it?' he said in a big, hearty, loud voice. I put the milk down carefully. He swept me up into his arms and kissed me on the cheek, a smacking kiss. He smelled of saddle soap and leather.

'Uncle Donald!' I said, when I found my voice.

'And you've grown up into a fine woman,' he said, still in that loud, hearty voice. 'But you seem surprised. Didn't you get my telegram?'

'Telegram?' I said.

'Never mind, I'm here now. Aren't you going to ask your uncle in for a cup of tea and a bit of family news?'

'Of course, Uncle, do come in. I'll just take the milk into the kitchen and go and wake Mum. She'll be so pleased to see you! And Dad's ill, did Mum say? He's outside in the backyard. Just put down that heavy thing in the parlour.'

I ran into Mum's room. She was already half awake.

'I hope it's a fire, Charlotte,' she said, only half joking.

'No, it's a brother,' said Uncle Donald, looking around the door. 'But I can go away again if I'm a trouble.'

Mum leapt out of bed and threw herself into his arms. 'Oh, Donnie,' she said. 'Oh, Donnie, is it really you?'

Uncle Donald told my mother that it was really him and I put the milk away. Mum was crying all down Uncle Donald's neck and I was embarrassed. I went out to tell Dad the good news and he grunted, 'Like a bad penny,' which was unfair because I thought he and Uncle Donald had always been friends. I tidied Dad a bit and picked up an envelope from under his chair. It was from a telegram. I looked at Dad. He had known that Uncle Donald was coming and hadn't told anyone. Why? I didn't say anything.

I counted the chickens, though. They were all still there.

Then I went and got sheets and made up the bed in the front room. This house belongs to Uncle Donald and Mum, and Uncle Donald's room is always kept ready for him. Mum and I had been airing it and dusting it for as long as I could remember. I knew every one of the trophies on his bookcase. I had washed and mended every one of his shirts. I hauled the swag into the room when I had finished the bed but it was too heavy for me to lift. I wondered what was in it. Lots of soldiers came home with things they had picked up in the war. Mrs Quilty's son had brought home a stuffed camel's hump from Cairo. She was very proud of it but it leaked sawdust. And Mrs Reilly's eldest son had sent her a lot of silk underwear from Paris, petticoats and chemises. She showed me the package when it came. They were beautiful, so soft.

I missed Dad and Uncle Donald meeting. When I came back to report that his room was ready Mum had made tea and Uncle Donald and Dad were sitting under the lemon tree side by side. Dad was trying to look happy. Mum was asking questions about the war and the trip home. Uncle Donald was telling her that it had all stopped at eleven o'clock, all the big guns, and then he had been sent straight to Boulogne and on a troop ship leaving for Australia.

'They didn't want us making any more trouble,' he said, grinning. 'They said we were the best troops and the worst behaved of all the Colonies. I only had two days for a look around London, then it was onto the ship and here I am. And very glad to be here,' he said, stretching his long legs and staring up at the sky. 'Peaceful here, eh, Alec?'

'Not if you're always listening to women screaming about nothing,' grunted Dad.

'Better that than shells screaming,' said Uncle Donald. 'Now, I'm going to have a bath and get changed. Want to come down to the baths, Charlotte?'

'Oh, Uncle, can't you stay like that until I can fetch the children home from next door? They'd love to see you in your uniform,' I said.

'Very well,' said Uncle Donald. 'But not one moment

49

after that, all right? I've been wearing this uniform for four years, and I'll be dashed if I wear it one moment longer than I have to.'

'Agreed,' I said. I raced next door to Florence's house and called them all to come and see Uncle Donald. Florence and her little sister Alice came too.

Albie was funny. He didn't remember Uncle Donald at all so he stood in the doorway while Amelia and Lily jumped into his lap and kissed him. Dad called him but Uncle Donald said, 'Let him get used to the idea, Alec,' and Albie drank Uncle Donald in from feathered hat to putteed boots. Then he made up his mind and jumped off the step straight into his arms. Uncle Donald only just caught him in time. Albie hung around his neck and laughed. Uncle Donald tossed him up into the air and caught him and Albie crowed with laughter.

Dad always used to toss Albie into the air like that. Mum had the same thought because she said, 'Look carefully, children, for Uncle Donald is going to get a bath and take off that uniform. And not put it on ever again, please God.'

'Amen,' said Uncle Donald.

I'm too excited to write any more.

18th December

Uncle Donald went to his room yesterday to find clothes to change into. I went too.

'Some little fairy has mended this shirt,' he said to me. 'And some little fairy has dusted my room and made my bed. Some busy little fairy has polished every one of those trophies. And some very hard working little fairy could do with some help in the house, couldn't she?'

I nodded. I didn't want to seem disloyal to Dad but I was very tired. He hadn't noticed all the things I had done for him. No one else did unless I didn't do them.

'Even fairies can do with some furlough,' said Uncle Donald. He took off all his badges, emptied his pockets, and took up an old felt hat. 'There, that's everything.'

Mum came in with a new comb and a cake of white soap. She was crying again. 'I've been saving this,' she said. 'I'm so glad you're home.'

'Another tired fairy,' said Uncle Donald. Then he kissed Mum and we went off to the baths. They were only two streets away. The swimming baths were at one end and the public baths at the other. We go there sometimes when it is a special occasion. The rest of the time we heat water on the stove and wash in a tin bath in front of the fire once a week.

Baths cost tuppence, towels cost a penny, but there is

endless hot water. I sat down in the office to wait for Uncle Donald and sniffed the steam. It had a faint carbolic smell. The man at the desk wouldn't let Uncle pay. He asked him about the troop ship and was overcome to find that his brother had been on it. After that he would have washed Uncle's back himself. He gave me a boiled lolly.

When Uncle Donald came back he was wearing his grey suit and a white shirt and holding his felt hat. He still looked twice as alive as anyone else in the room. He hefted the bag, which had his uniform in it, and we went out into the street. He crooked his elbow and I put my hand on his arm, like a lady. I was very proud of my handsome uncle.

On the way home he went into the grocer's and ordered a lot of food. Then we went into the pub (or rather, he did and I stayed outside) and he ordered some bottled beer and a bottle of Queensland rum. I heard the men in the pub call his name and invite him to have a drink with them but he told them he was escorting a young lady and couldn't stop. Then he came out in a cloud of beer and sawdust smell and asked me what the children would like as a treat. I said ice-cream and he grinned and said that he was glad that some things didn't change.

So Florence and Alice and Lily and Mum and Amelia and Albie and me all walked down to the greengrocer's shop and my saintly Uncle Donald produced a handful of silver and we all had our favourite, fruit ice blocks with cream.

It has been a lovely day. Even better because Uncle Donald told Lily that he would buy a turkey for Christmas and her chickens were safe. She introduced him to all of them by name. And dinner was a lot of tinned things: salmon and sardines and Camp Pie (Albie loved this and Uncle Donald let him eat most of it) and ham and eggs and toast and peaches and glacé cherries and shop cake. After that Mum gave us all a dose of milk of magnesia and sent us to bed.

I'm so glad Uncle Donald has come home.

19th December

Dispensary was crowded tonight. There were people sitting outside on the fence when I came in with my clean apron and my linen cap. Mrs Thomas arrived late for her usual dressing and said there was a man lying on the road. Dr Barnes went out to find out what had happened.

When he came back two men were carrying another. I finished with Mrs Thomas and she patted me on the head and I went to my place at the doctor's side.

The man's face was blue. Blue as a gun barrel. Blue

as a thundercloud. I had never seen a human face that colour.

'He's drowning,' said Dr Barnes, which seemed strange because the patient was on dry land. 'You, Miss Mac, hand me that scalpel and get these fellows out of here. Then unbutton his shirt.'

I did as I was bid. I showed the men out and closed the door. Then I held a basin as Dr Barnes plunged the scalpel into the patient's chest and liquid poured out. Clear, frothy liquid. He told me to pour it away while he turned the man over. Every breath wheezed out of the poor man, but the blue seemed to ebb a little. More fluid. Another basinful. The patient coughed and spat and drew an easier breath.

'That's why you said he was drowning,' I remarked.

'From the inside,' he agreed. 'Charlotte, I know you have had the influenza. How about the rest of your family?'

'None of them,' I said.

'Then before you go home you must wash all over, dress in clean clothes, and leave these here to wear next time. Gargle with a one-in-sixteen carbolic wash. And wash your hair in carbolic soap. I shall do the same,' he added. 'Florence can lend you something to go home in,' he said. 'But you mustn't go near her until you are clean.'

I told him I wouldn't. Then he said that the patient must go to hospital and asked if he was the last. I told him there were still people waiting.

'Tell them from the door that they must either go to

the hospital or come back tomorrow,' he ordered. A lady said that her baby seemed better and she would come back tomorrow. Old Mrs Flowers was annoyed. She said she had come for another bottle of the tonic and she was going to get it. I told Doctor and he said to fill her bottle before I left, so I did. She went away, very cross.

'She only needs that tonic because it's one-third good medicinal alcohol,' snorted the Doctor. 'You can have the bathroom first, Miss Mac.'

I had never been in a bathroom which was just for washing and where the water came out of a tap hot. I nearly scalded myself, playing with it. Florence called from the door and said she had left me some clothes and to put mine in a bucket of carbolic. I hoped my printed calico would stand the treatment.

Then I dried myself and put on Florence's cotton dress and drawers and my own shoes, which had been swabbed. It was a nice dress, pale green. Florence has red hair (auburn, she says) so she can't wear pink, which is a mercy. I hate pink.

Florence grabbed me when I came out.

'What's happening?' she asked, hugging me. 'Father is so stern! He said he'd beat me if I came in to see you before you were washed. Father never says things like that.'

'He's afraid that you might catch the flu,' I told her. 'Don't worry, Florence.'

I hugged her back and suddenly felt very, very much older than my friend.

When I got home I told Uncle Donald and he said that they had had the flu on the Front in May. 'The Frenchies called it *la grippe*,' he said. 'Three days of aches and pains and then we got better. I never even caught it. Don't worry, little fairy. That's a new dress, isn't it? It suits you. Go and look in the ice-box,' he added. 'We saved some for you, though it was a tussle with young Albie here.'

There was a dish of ice-cream in the ice-box. It was a bit runny, but it tasted divine.

I don't think that Uncle Donald's flu and the one which had turned that poor man's face as black as a cast-iron stove were the same things. And I have never seen Doctor Barnes so worried.

20th December

It's ten in the morning. Mum's let me off doing the floor because I'm writing my diary—so I'd better write.

Outside my little window, Dad sits watching Uncle Donald play football with Albie and he looks so strange, so pinched and mean that I can't bear to look at him.

But having Uncle Donald here is lovely. He's got his

back pay and he is thinking about what he means to do. He says he has enough to start a business. The Government is offering land to returned soldiers, but Uncle Donald says he's had enough of the land.

'I've had it on me and under me and over me and I've swallowed quite a lot of France. I want a business where I only have to walk on good old asphalt and smell good healthy petrol fumes. I want a roof over my head and a soft bed and a pub within reach and a few old mates to have a yarn. Out there in the backblocks there's no one to talk to but trees,' he said, and Lily giggled.

Mum is much happier since he came home. She's been smiling. He's such a funny man. And this morning when I came back from fetching Dad's medicine and was about to start cleaning the kitchen, I heard the sound of sandsoap scrubbing wood. I found Uncle Donald, in a pair of overalls, working on the kitchen table. He'd already cleaned, blacked and polished the stove and he must have worked very fast because the floor was already nearly dry.

'Housework's hard work,' he said. 'G'day, Charlotte! I've nearly finished this. Get me a beer and an opener and meet me under the lemon tree.'

I did as he bade me and he came out into the yard and sat down in the mended chair, opened the bottle and took a deep swig.

'Uncle, where did you learn to do housework?' I asked, amazed.

'I was an orderly for a while,' he said. 'In a hospital in London. And didn't that Matron go crook if we didn't flog her floors spotless enough to suit her fancy! You remember, Alec?'

Dad grunted. Uncle Donald paid no attention to his rudeness and went on, 'And you could have eaten your dinner off them floors when we finished with 'em. Little house like this isn't hardly worth botherin' about. Though if you really want hygiene, you need a sailor. They live so cheek-by-jowl that they've got to be neat. Eh, Alec?'

Dad grunted again. Uncle Donald ignored his response and kept trying to talk to him. They made a striking contrast, sitting side by side. Dad crouched in his dressing gown, shrunken and pale, and Uncle Donald, legs stretched out, head back, drinking beer from the bottle, so healthy and strong.

I felt sorry for Dad, suddenly, and had to go inside and do the dusting.

21st December

The food is all ordered for Christmas dinner.

Just after noon yesterday a carrier came from the Railways and brought us a big box. Uncle Donald carried it inside and took it into the yard. He'd knocked up a garden table and he set the box on it.

'Come along, Alec,' he said. 'You open it. It's for you.'

Dad tottered over and watched as Uncle Donald wrenched off the wooden lid. We all said, 'Ah!' A beautiful, fruity, spicy smell wafted up and Dad smiled.

'Christmas pudding,' he said. 'It's from Mum.'

Grandma McKenzie lives in Hamilton, where Dad was born. We don't see her often. She's an alarming old lady, very abrupt. I'm rather scared of her. But she makes the Christmas pudding every year because Mum is working. There were other things in the box, wrapped in brown paper, with labels. Dad set them out on the table.

'Presents,' he said. 'You can put them in the parlour, children. Make sure Albie doesn't open his. Good heavens, Don, there's one for you. How did she know you'd be home?'

'She's Scottish,' said Uncle Donald, taking up his parcel and poking it. 'They've got second sight. Or so the Cameron Highlanders always said. Good fighters, but. That's very nice of the old lady,' he told Dad.

In the bottom of the box were bottles of preserved peaches and apricots and cherries. I lined them up in the pantry. They sparkled.

I also poked my parcel. It was squashy. I put all the parcels but one under our Christmas tree. It isn't a live tree. It's a dead branch painted silver with tinsel and coloured balls. Lily and Amelia put Albie's small, heavy parcel out of reach on the mantelpiece. Then they took him for a walk when he screeched.

I put the pudding on the clean, dry kitchen shelf.

The turkey came in the afternoon. Poor Jimmy, the grocer's boy, staggered under the weight of it. It was huge.

'That'll never fit in our oven,' I said to Uncle Donald.

'Trust your Uncle to have thought of that,' he said, and bore it off. He was away for hours. When he came back we had tea.

Dad had been getting worse all day. When we had finished tea and cleared away and washed the dishes, Mum sent us into the parlour. I read some of my school prize, Lily played with her doll, Albie played with his tin-can trains and Amelia sat under the lamp, finishing her Christmas presents. It was very quiet. We could hear Mrs Barnes playing her phonograph. Dad and Uncle Donald were sitting out under the lemon tree. Mum was doing something in the kitchen which we were not to know about but I could hear the rustling of paper. She has two and a half day's off at Christmas so she can sleep in tomorrow.

23rd December

Lots more happened last night. I took notes. I'm writing this as though it was a story, but it all happened just as I shall relate.

It was a nice quiet evening. Gradually we all went to bed. First Albie. He put up his usual fight about having his face washed—why do boys love dirt so?—but we won in the end. Then Lily, then Amelia. Finally there was only me. I tiptoed out, kissed Mum good night, then went out into the yard and into my little room. I washed my face and hands and put on my nightgown. I didn't light my candle because they're expensive and anyway, I could manage perfectly well. There was a full moon, almost as bright as day.

Then I realised I could hear voices.

Dad and Uncle Donald were sitting with their chairs almost against the wall of my room. The door is on the other side and they might not have noticed I was there. I didn't know what to do. Should I cough to let them know I could hear them?

I didn't cough. I took out my diary and wrote down what they said.

Dad said, 'You've come out of the war all right, Don.'

'No one comes out of the war all right, Alec,' said Uncle Donald quietly.

'Look at you!' said Dad. 'Tall, healthy, fit as a scrub bull. And look at me.'

'You copped it,' said Uncle Donald. 'Lots of us copped it.'

'Yes, and they're dead,' said Dad. 'The lucky bastards.'

'Where did it happen?' asked Uncle Donald, ignoring this.

'Villers-Brettoneux,' said Dad after a pause.

'It was a bad show, they say,' said Uncle Donald. Dad laughed. It was not a nice laugh. Uncle went on, 'Buried, were you, Alec?'

'Eleven hours,' said Dad. 'I could hear them tramping overhead, like I was already dead. They only found me because they were digging for a cable. Shovel blade went into my leg and I yelled.'

'No one comes out of that all right,' said Uncle.

'Only reason I didn't drown in mud was I had my head in an air pocket. The bloke above me went down cut in half and I was . . . between . . .' Dad gulped.

'Shouldn't happen to a dog, Alec,' said Uncle.

'Sent me to London. Whole ward full of shakers and screamers. Said I was a nut case and sent me home with my tail between my legs,' Dad went on.

So he had been buried. Mum was right.

Then Uncle said, 'Got nightmares, Alec?'

'Have you?' snarled Dad.

'Of course,' said Uncle. 'We've all got the nightmares, Alec. The shakes.'

'What happened to you?' asked Dad. It was the first question he had asked Uncle Donald since he came home.

'Opened up by a shell fragment,' said Uncle. I heard him unbuttoning his shirt. Dad gasped. 'I even made the stretcher bearers sick. They piled my insides back and sent me down the line. I had peritonitis. They didn't think I'd live. I spent six months in a convalescent home, living on junket. No stuff for a grown man. But I'm strong. There were times when I wished I wasn't. Then they sent me back.'

'That was hard,' said Dad.

'The worst thing, Alec, is that we went out with dreams of glory and, by the time we found out it was all mud and murder and rats, it was too late. We were in at the start and we were in at the end, but it was cruel work. And we've all got the horrors. Those blokes skiting about how much they loved the war—they're lying or they're fools.'

'Or they never got further than Headquarters,' said Dad.

'Four miles behind the Front,' said Uncle.

Dad actually chuckled. I heard Uncle Donald pour some more of the Queensland rum into his glass. I could smell burned sugar.

'And you can't tell them,' said Uncle. 'First because

it's too awful, then because they wouldn't believe it, and then . . .'

'Because you'd have to tell the whole story,' said Dad. 'Too many horrors. We fought the war to keep them safe from horrors.'

'And we have,' said Uncle. 'But we took them on ourselves and we'll never be free of them, Alec. Only difference between us is my wound's on the outside, yours is on the inside. I was so low in that hospital that I stole a flask of sleeping draught. I spent days thinking about doing myself in. Then I thought of you, and Alice, and the kids, and Eddie, and I didn't.'

'So we're both hurt,' said Dad. 'What was it for?'

'I dunno, mate,' said Uncle Donald. 'I got back and saw the hungry kids in Footscray and the worn out women and I dunno. World's changing. We just have to do the best we can.'

'Not a lot I can do,' said Dad. He sounded angry.

'I got an idea about that,' said Uncle. 'About this business I'm thinking of starting.'

'How can you?' cried Dad. 'You were there. You saw it—the mud and the lice and the depths men can sink to.'

'I was there,' said Uncle softly. 'And I saw the heights they can rise to. I won't have it said that we came home and dropped our bundle, Alec. I won't have it. We have to make a world fit for our children, because sure as eggs, no one is going to do it for us.'

'That's true,' said Dad.

They were silent for a while. Then Uncle said, 'What do they say about your health, Alec?'

'Said no one knows about shell shock. Repat won't pay me much of a pension. One said I was malingering.'

'He said that?'

'No, he offered me two aspirins,' snarled Dad.

Uncle began to laugh, and after a moment, of all things, Dad began to laugh too.

'So they don't know if you can get better?' asked Uncle Donald.

'No,' said Dad. 'No one knows.'

'Then why not see what you can do?' asked Uncle. 'You can stop when you're tired. Just get dressed and come down to the baths with me tomorrow. Stop grubbing about in slippers and dressing gown. You used to like swimming.'

'You're going swimming?' asked Dad. 'With that scar?'

'I'm game if you are,' said Uncle.

There was a long pause.

'Done,' said Dad. 'Got a bit more of that Queensland poison for an old digger?'

Uncle Donald laughed. Then we heard Mrs Barnes's phonograph. She was playing 'There's a Long Long Trail a-Winding'.

Uncle Donald started singing along: 'Where the

nightingale is singing and the bright moon beams'. And I think—I don't know, because I couldn't see—but I think my Dad was crying.

Tomorrow is Christmas Eve!

24th December

We've all been scurrying about, cleaning the house so it will be nice for Christmas. Uncle Donald and Dad got up early and went to the swimming baths. Dad actually put shoes on and didn't get angry when he found out that moths had got at his socks. Florence told me to keep the pale green dress, she's got lots. I ironed it by myself on the kitchen table. Flat irons are very heavy and it's very hard to make sure that they haven't got any soot from the stove. And then, just when you've got them clean, they cool down so you have to put them back on the stove again and they get sooty. But I did iron the dress and I've got a new green hair ribbon. So have Lily and Amelia; pale pink for Lily and pale blue for Amelia. Florence's dress is the nicest dress I have ever had.

Mum brought some holly home from the hospital and Amelia made red berries out of clay. She also made white berries for the mistletoe, though it's a branch of ivy really. Mistletoe doesn't grow around here. She also made a wreath for the door. Amelia's so clever at hand crafts. I'm not, so I washed all the good plates and glasses and cups and saucers and the big china serving dish that came with Great-Grandma from England.

Uncle Donald evened out the wobble in the dining room table and then said, 'Why sit inside? Let's take it outside,' and he and Dad did, so we had to have tea in the kitchen.

It's fine dry weather and the yard looks different since Uncle Donald has been tidying it. Lily's chooks are shut in their run at night now and he's cut back the ivy, trimmed a couple of branches off the lemon tree so you can sit under it without banging your head, and mowed the grass. It looks more like a garden. Mum's geraniums were still alive under all that couch grass and they're flowering, bright red and pink and white. Uncle Donald said that he'll plant climbing roses on the fences when the right time comes and that will be lovely.

The weather continues fair and warm. I hope it won't rain tomorrow.

25th December

I had been wondering about that turkey. Uncle Donald went off with it and came back hours later. How far had he taken it? Would it come back in time for Christmas dinner? Mum and me laid the table and it looked lovely, though we had to tell Sable that it wasn't a nice place for a cat to sleep. We had the special damask tablecloth that belonged to Great-Grandma and all the silver and the plates and cups shone bright in the sun.

For some reason I didn't sleep very well and I was feeling not very Christmassy but we were all pleased with our presents. Grandma McKenzie had knitted each of us a jumper out of brightly coloured wool, even one for Uncle Donald. The little hard parcel for Albie proved to be a splendid tin boat, with a little space for a candle and a real boiler. Albie was so pleased that Uncle filled the tin bath and Mum took off most of Albie's holiday clothes and put on his old overalls and he spent the morning watching his ship putt-putt up and down the water. He got very wet and was very happy. I gave Lily her pearl beads and she put them on at once. Mum liked her hanky and so did Dad. Amelia had embroidered me a cover for my washstand, made Lily a beautiful embroidered blouse and slippers for Uncle Donald and Dad. Mum has a newly trimmed hat and Albie a cross-stitch shirt for holidays.

The best presents were from Uncle Donald but Dad didn't seem to be cross about this. Mum had some perfume called 'Jicky' which came from Paris. It smelled wonderful, like a whole flower-garden. I have a white silk petticoat, Lily has a wonderful doll called Jeanne, and

Amelia has a sewing box with a padded lid and places for all her projects. It has spools of thread and needles and a pair of scissors shaped like a swan. She adores it. I put on the petticoat and it swishes. It feels lovely. I would rather have had a book, though, but I couldn't say that to Uncle Donald. He gave my father a pouch of pipe tobacco which smells like honey.

Mum and Dad gave us each a box of toffees. Then Florence came over and gave me a book, *Robinson Crusoe*. I can't wait to read it. I gave her the cedar box I had made, for handkerchiefs. Dad had showed me how to do it but I had done it all myself, even though he was cross and said that it was no fit work for a girl. I love working with wood. It smells so nice. The box has Florence's name burned into the top in poker-work. Florence said that Dr Barnes sent a present for 'Miss Mac, his able assistant'. It was a library subscription.

Now I can borrow two books a week from Miss Jones's Lending Library. A wonderful present.

But where was the turkey? The potatoes and peas were ready and the plates set out when Uncle Donald vanished with the big china plate and came back with the turkey, all perfectly cooked and shiny and crispy-skinned, with a pot of gravy. He'd asked Mrs Reilly to cook it for us, along with the Barnes's Christmas dinner. Dad stuck a fork into it and it streamed stuffing, sage and onion.

Then we all ate turkey and gravy and potatoes and

peas until we really didn't think we had any room left, except that when the pudding came out of the copper and Mum peeled off the cloth it smelled so heavenly that we all had some with brandy sauce, and then we all lay down for a little sleep, except Albie, who was sick first.

In the afternoon we played with our presents and the grown-ups drank sherry and talked. I was so lazy and happy that I kept falling asleep and pinching myself because I wanted to stay awake and enjoy everything: Lily explaining to her doll Belinda that Jeanne was a visitor and it didn't mean that she loved Belinda any less; Albie back in the yard watching his steam ship putt-putting up and down the bath; Lily combing out her long hair and trying it in different styles; Amelia squeaking every time she found a fresh surprise in her sewing box; Mum looking pink and cheerful; Dad talking about the football to Uncle Donald; and Uncle Donald leaning back in his chair and smiling.

We were very happy today. It's dark now and I'm in my own room. We had a light tea of turkey sandwiches and Dad and Uncle Donald had beer. They've all gone to bed. No one is awake but me, and I'm only awake because I don't want to go to sleep in case I lose this warm feeling that everything really is going to be all right.

But that's the fourth blot I've made. Good night.

28th December

It's always a little sad after Christmas is all over but I'm not sad to see the last of that turkey. We have had it hot then cold and then made into rissoles and finally the bones went for soup.

Today is very hot. Dad went to the swimming baths with Uncle Donald. He's starting to look better. He doesn't stoop so much and he's not wearing slippers all day. And he can't sit over the fire, because it's too hot. I don't like the heat. I keep trying to persuade Mum to have salads. Uncle Donald bought us a primus stove. A great convenience. We can boil a kettle without having to light the fire in the stove, which heats up the whole house. It was one hundred degrees Fahrenheit today. The only one who loves the heat is Lily. And even Lily was a bit droopy today.

We went down to the beach on the train with Uncle Donald. We all had to wear our shirts because the sun was so hot, but Albie got a bit burned. When we came home Mum put calamine lotion on him and he went around being a ghost. There was lemonade out of the ice-box. It was a lovely day.

1st January 1919

Wednesday. It's a new year! We were allowed to sit up until midnight. Albie and Lily fell asleep, sitting out on the back veranda in the dark, but Amelia and I stayed awake. So did Mum and Uncle Donald. Dad fell asleep in his chair. I heard Mum say to Uncle Donald, 'How is he?' meaning Dad, and Uncle Donald said in his slow voice, 'Coming along, Alice, coming along.'

It was a hot night and the mosquitoes were bad. Mum burned a citronella candle which kept them away. It was exciting, sitting in the dark, with nothing but the little point of the candle. Voices sound different in the dark. Faces look different in candle light.

I was thinking about Uncle Donald lying so dreadfully wounded that he made the stretcher bearers sick and Dad being buried under mud for eleven hours. They don't want us to know what the horrors of war are. They want to keep us safe. But I don't want to be so safe that I have to be ignorant. If I had understood what Dad was remembering I wouldn't have been so cross with him.

Then we heard the bell from the church. It has a striking clock and it began to toll, twelve times, midnight. Then all the other bells joined in. Mum, Dad, Amelia, Uncle Donald and me joined hands and sang

'For Auld Lang Syne'. Then we drank a toast to the new year.

'May it be better than the old!' said Mum, and we all agreed.

Then we went to bed. Uncle Donald watched me go into my little room and close the door and I could see him thinking about his talk with Dad and how, from my room I could have overheard it. But he didn't say anything and I lit my candle. Then he grinned and waved good night. Of course. If I had been there he would have seen the light.

If that's what Uncle Donald thinks, I know better. And I'm not saying anything. If people won't tell me things, then I shall have to find out for myself.

5th January 1919

I have to write 1919 because I'm so used to 1918 that I keep writing it. And I haven't written in my diary for a few days because there has been nothing special that's happened.

It's dark and hot. Dr Barnes has asked if I will come with him on his morning rounds, starting tomorrow. That poor man he had at his Dispensary just before Christmas died in hospital. Lots of people are down with this flu.

This means a lot of washing as I cannot come back into my family's house unless I have been disinfected.

Dr Barnes says he wants me with him because he is on the road so long every day that he is afraid that he will fall asleep and steer the pony cart into the ditch. This is silly because Bethesda, his mare, will bring him home just as she always does. I once saw her come clopping around to the front door with the doctor fast asleep in the driver's seat and the reins knotted around the bar. When he didn't move she whinnied and stamped and Mike, the houseman, woke up and came to help.

I don't know why Doctor wants me but I am another pair of hands, I suppose. And he's going to pay me fourteen shillings a week. That's almost what Dad gets on his pension. Now I come to write that down it seems strange and unfair. I didn't have to be buried eleven hours to get fourteen shillings a week.

But the money will be very helpful and Mum can get Mrs Quilty to come in for the heavy housework. Mum says I should keep five shillings a week for myself. I don't know what I am to do with so much money. Perhaps I can save it. I will need uniforms and things when I begin as a nurse. I know probationer nurses only get paid two shillings and sixpence a week, though they live in at the hospital and are fed and lodged. And their uniforms and things are washed there. Still it seems a lot of money.

6th January

I'm finally home and I'm so tired I can hardly hold a pen. I am writing this down because I want to be good at my trade, medicine, and to do that I must have case notes. I'll write as much as I can and then I'll continue early tomorrow before I go out with the doctor again.

The flu is spreading, though mostly in the poorer houses where people live close together. Dr Barnes thinks it might spread by contact, and some of the houses I have seen today are so small and have so many people living in them that the people must be in contact with someone all the time.

Dr Barnes had a list of all the people who needed a doctor. Bethesda trotted off to the first house, which was quite close. The weather was still cool because it was only seven in the morning. The door was shut fast and Doctor knocked and called without an answer. Then we saw that the milk in the billy was curdled solid. So Doctor set his shoulder to the door and shoved and it swung open. A dreadful smell rushed out. I put on my mask. It is made of three layers of gauze dipped in carbolic, so all you can smell is carbolic, which is an improvement.

There was a man lying on the floor just inside the door. The doctor turned him over. He was dead. He was the first dead man I had ever seen.

I had wondered how I would manage seeing dead people. It was not horrible. If he had not been that terrible colour he would not have looked strange. But he was blue, almost black. Dr Barnes pushed the body aside and stepped over him into the house. As I came closer I felt that it was cruel to just step over him as though he was nothing but the doctor called me and I went. I told the dead man I was sorry.

Then I followed the doctor into the inner room. It was a two-roomed house. Three children were huddled together, crying. A woman lay in a bed on the floor. She was alive and so was her baby, which was wailing.

The doctor bade me clean up, boil water, feed the children and open the back door and the window. I started with the window. There was no opening it; it was stuck fast with paint and dirt. The eldest boy told me that Dad was sick and in the front room. I didn't know what to say about the dead man so I told him to bring his little brothers into the kitchen. I managed to light the stove, which had not quite gone out, and scour a pot clean enough to put water in. The only water came from a tap in the backyard and a water barrel which was green with slime.

Feeding the children was a problem. There was nothing in the pantry but a scrap of old cheese and the remains of a loaf of bread. In a paper bag I found a pinch of tea but no milk and nothing else but rot and dust. I had thought that we were poor. We were rich. We always had something to eat.

Using the cleanest of the rags I found, I washed the children's faces and hands and felt their foreheads. They did not seem to be hot. Under the dirt they looked thin but healthy. I took my pot of hot water into the other room and Doctor told me to wash the woman and the baby. When I said there was nothing to eat and no soap, he told me to look in the cart.

In the back of the trap I found a large pot of soup, a basket full of cleaning things and seven loaves of bread. I carried these things inside and set about feeding the children. I don't think they saw real bread and soup very often because they almost tore the food out of my hands and each one fled into a corner to eat it by himself. I sent them out into the yard while I tried to wash the woman.

Her skin was so hot that I thought the water would steam off it. Her eyes were half open and she was dragging in racking breaths. I managed to sponge most of her without spilling too much, for she was unable to help me. Then I ransacked the house and found one clean sheet, which I wrapped around her.

The baby was hot and unhappy. He was probably hungry. I didn't have any milk so I fed him some cooled broth. His little gums snapped around the spoon. There was no clean nappy for him so I used a rag. Then I swept out the house. I had to sweep round the dead man because he was too heavy for me to move. The doctor had gone out to find someone to send for the undertaker. The broom only had about three straws left. I might have washed the floor but I would have had to move the body.

Cleaning the house had only taken about half an hour. It had no furniture.

The doctor came back and said he had sent a message for the undertaker and he wrote out a certificate. He also brought a thin, scared woman, Mrs Benson, from next door who said that she would mind the children until the Welfare arrived. She went in past the corpse with a shriek and begged the doctor to hurry. The children seemed to know her.

Then we packed up and went on.

'All right, Miss Mac?' the doctor asked me.

'All right,' I replied. I think I spoke the truth.

The next house was four streets down. There we saw a door painted a cheerful shade of yellow and a pot of geraniums by it. A man let us in.

'She's worse,' he said.

We went inside and found a woman who was wailing, a horrible, high, thin shriek. She was brushing at the sheet, which was very white, and saying, 'Spiders, spiders! John, chase them away, chase them, spiders, John,' over and over again. Doctor told the husband to keep giving her aspirin and water and he would call in the evening. Her temperature was 105 degrees, almost at the top of the thermometer. I dipped it in carbolic solution and tried again but it was still 105. She never stopped begging her husband to come and kill the spiders. The husband was laying a cloth soaked in lavender water on her forehead and it dried almost at once.

I asked the doctor about aspirin as we started the trap for the next address. He told me it was a wonderful new invention. 'Reduces fever, relieves pain. And it's cheap. Professor Bayer, who invented it, wouldn't patent it because it was a boon to the world, so it's not expensive. But even modern medicine can't do much for this flu, Miss Mac. I'm making money like I never did, and I wish I was poor.'

'What was in the blue bottle, then?' I asked. The sun was getting bright and I shaded my eyes as Bethesda clopped over the cobbles into a street which ran east-west.

'A tonic,' said the doctor. 'A little flavouring and some bergamot extract. What is the first principle of Hippocrates, the first doctor, Miss Mac?'

I was so proud of myself. I knew this one. 'Do no harm,' I said.

'Keep it in mind,' he said, 'when you follow me today. I can't cure the flu. I wish I could. All I can do is comfort the stricken. Put your mask on, Miss Mac, this is going to be a bad one.'

If the dead man in the first house hadn't been bad, I wondered, what was bad in Dr Barnes's eyes? I put on my mask and folded my hands together, in case they wanted to shake.

The next stop was a boarding house, and Dr Barnes was right. It reminded me more of a sermon I had heard about Hell, when Florence and I sneaked out to a Baptist chapel. We had been frightened into good behaviour for weeks afterwards.

All the adults in the house were sick. There was a white cloth tied to the front gate, which meant that they had the flu. But, as always, I expected that the strong healthy people would be able to resist the infection and the children and old people would be stricken. That is the way that Dr Barnes had explained the flu to me.

But this flu was picking the people who would usually be the nurses and the cooks and the cleaners.

I smelled it even through the carbolic mask. A terrible reek of sickness, a flu smell that I racked my brains to compare to anything. Wet mice was the closest I got. It was a sickly, half-sweet smell a little like the blood on meat which your mother has decided may do for a stew if she wipes it with vinegar first. Combined with a musky smell like old cheese. It feels like I will never get that smell out of my nose.

The boarding house had ten rooms. Each one had

more than one tenant. One room had seven people in it and the only one who didn't have the flu was an old man. He was lying in the corner and I thought he might be dead so I pushed his shoulder and he rolled over and belched. Doctor Barnes chuckled as a rich smell of port came to his nose.

'That one's just drunk,' he said. 'You leave him where he is, m'dear. He's drunk his own punishment. And this baby is healthy, though hungry. We will have to find someone to look after these people, Miss Mac. There's too many of them for us alone.'

I did not tell him that the prospect of cleaning that house filled me with dread. It wasn't just the flu, the awful fluids on the floor and the lack of ventilation. That place hadn't been scoured since, as Grandma McKenzie would say, Adam was a boy. It was filthy with a rubbed in grime which nothing short of a fire hose and a City Council broom could hope to remove.

But we saw every person, gave them all boiled water or soup and checked their temperature. It was always terribly high. I thought that 107 was a killing fever, but three people here had it and were still alive. Doctor talked to all of them, even those who could not hear him, gently and reassuringly, and he finally roused the drunk with a bucket of water in the face. He sat up, very indignant, with water dripping from his beard. 'Get up and help, you sot,' roared Dr Barnes, and quite chastened—he may have thought Dr Barnes was an alarming vision—he started to mop floors and re-lit the stove.

The Irishwoman in the top room was already dead, but her two-year-old child was still alive and not even hot, though his mother showed the black face and the black feet. I brought the child downstairs with the offer of some food. He was very hungry, poor little chap, but he let me feed him soup with bread broken into it. His mouth gaped like a little bird's.

Were they all going to die? What had happened to the world? Was this a punishment from God for starting the war?

We left the little boy with the drunken man, who had taken over the kitchen and was making porridge. He said he was the child's father. I don't know how that could be, since he was lying drunk in quite another room, but it was not for me to say, as long as someone fed the child. Dr Barnes sent a boy in the street for the undertaker and we went on.

We found one valiant little girl who had washed and cared for her sisters. She had even tried to make soup but it had spilt and put the stove out. It spilt because she couldn't reach the top of the stove even standing on a chair. She was eight.

I managed to relight the fire and found a smaller pot so she could see into it. Her father was a big heavy man and it took me and the doctor and the child to shove him into bed. He was delirious and thought he had to get up and go to work. Doctor ordered him to stay in bed because it was a holiday, and he sank back and closed his eyes.

The child told me her name was Matty. She was so brave. Her mother had the flu as well. She wasn't restless. She had sunk into a deep sleep and the doctor had hopes that she might recover and promised to send someone to help Matty before the end of the day.

'Did you study Latin, Miss Mac?' the doctor asked me as Bethesda trotted along to the next house.

'Yes, Doctor,' I answered.

'How would you translate *novus morbus*?' he asked.

'New disease,' I answered.

'That, I fear, m'girl, is what we have,' he said, and didn't say anything else until we were at the next house.

This wasn't a house at all but a tent on some waste land near the railway. I could hear someone counting, 'One, two, three, four,' but there was something mechanical about the voice, as if a clock had a voice. A ragged man grabbed the doctor by the arm. The doctor did not shake him off.

I had to bend double to get into the tent. In it was a young man of about twenty and an older man. Both had the high fever and it was the young man who was counting. They were lying on beds made of branches but they were tended and clean and straw was laid under the beds, which another old man had just finished changing as we arrived.

'Comfortable enough,' said the doctor. Indeed the tent was much cooler and more airy than that boarding house. He gave the old man a bottle of the blue medicine and a paper of aspirin powders. 'I'll be back tonight,' he said. 'See how much boiled water you can get them to drink. One of these every four hours.'

'I'll light a fire directly,' said the old man. Doctor took his temperature and it was normal.

'It's the vengeance of God,' said the old man. 'My son and my grandson.'

'The vengeance is on all of us, then,' said Dr Barnes. 'Rich and poor alike, guilty and innocent. I'll be back before dark,' he promised. 'Keep up your heart. Don't give up,' he added, as we trotted away.

It was time to stop and put Bethesda's nosebag on. We stopped in the middle of the park. Carts were not allowed in these but no one stopped Dr Barnes from going where he liked and everyone knew Bethesda.

'Our nosebag is under the seat,' said the doctor. I opened a hamper and it in were chicken sandwiches and little cakes with icing. I couldn't touch a bite. Doctor Barnes looked annoyed but I really wasn't hungry.

'Mrs Reilly thought you might like this,' he said, and

produced a flask of clear, salty, beef broth. It went down very well, and after that I ate two sandwiches and a cake.

Dr Barnes and I had cold, sweet tea from a bottle. There was only one cup and he insisted that I take it. It felt strange, sitting on a park seat next to the munching pony, drinking cold tea. Almost like a picnic. I suppose it was like a picnic in Hell. If they have picnics there.

I must be falling asleep. I always repeat myself when I'm tired. But when I write it down it hurts less. Once written down it is a different sort of real.

When we went on with the rest of the calls, it was always the same pattern. Doctor said that if we saw an old person and a baby on the porch it meant the flu and so it proved.

The next house was in a nice street. There was the white pillowcase tied to the letterbox, saying the flu is here. In *Stories from the Lives of Noble Women* they used to put a black cross on the door if they had the plague and the words 'Lord Have Mercy Upon Us'. Here one ties a white cloth to the front gate as a warning that no one may enter. Except Dr Barnes and me.

This house had a woman and a man, both with terrible temperatures, and a little boy about five and an old lady quite untouched. But the old lady was saying that they must send a nurse. 'I can't wash; that is servant's work. I can't cook, I never learned; that's cook's work.'

Dr Barnes shouted at her that she must work or her

children would die. 'If you can't cook, they only need water and soup. If you can't wash, then they'll lie in filthy linen.' She seemed to gather herself together and called the doctor a common rascal to speak so to a lady and he laughed and told her he'd be back that night.

It went on and on. In one house a girl was weeping as though her heart would break because her wedding dress wasn't ready and she was getting married the next day. Her mother told us that she was about to be married but her groom had been struck down and so had she. She shook her head over the idea of her daughter marrying anyone. We gave her some aspirin and said we'd be back.

The worst thing is that all the people who don't usually get the flu are getting it and there is no one to look after them but old people and children.

One house was odd. Even for the sort of day I had it was odd. They didn't have the flu. Three soldiers lived there together and one had a broken leg.

'You can't send him to hospital,' protested the one who did all the talking. 'People only go to hospital to die these days.'

'Very well,' said the doctor, who was as pleased as I was to see someone who didn't have the flu. 'Miss Mac, bring in an ether mask and the bottle of ether, the plaster of paris and the bandages.'

The way we set the leg was like this. We laid the patient out on the kitchen table. I stood at his head with the ether mask, which looks like a big tea strainer, over his nose and mouth. It has eight layers of muslin in it and I had to drip one drop of ether on it every minute, so I missed some of the operation because I was counting. I had already mixed the plaster and laid out the bandages. The broken leg looked horrible. It had been fractured across the shin but the doctor said that the bone was broken simply and it should be easy to reduce, which is the medical word for putting it back where it belonged.

Then he just took the man's foot in his hand and moved the leg until he could feel that the bone was in place and all the muscles were lying correctly. It made a grating noise, but I was counting my ether and tried not to listen.

Then the doctor had the man's smaller mate hold it steady while he wound plaster bandages around the leg and under the foot. These were secured with a knot.

Then all we had to do was wait for the plaster to set, which it did very fast on such a hot day.

'Remove the ether mask,' said Doctor, so I took it away and corked the bottle. This was a relief, because that heavy smell was making me dizzy. I gathered up all our belongings and cleaned up while Dr Barnes stood holding the patient's heel in his hand to make sure the leg was extended.

'Bad show,' said the doctor. 'How did he break his leg?'

'Drunk,' said the bigger mate. 'Stumbled over Pat here in the dark.'

Pat was the dog. He wagged his tail, not sure if this was all his fault. The doctor patted him and then knocked his knuckles on the cast. It gave back a dull sound.

'Well, that feels all right. We'll just sit down until he recovers. Mind that, Miss Mac. Never assume that anyone is going to come well out of anaesthesia.'

I said that I understood. Luckily, too, because when the man came around he leapt off the table and raced outside to be sick, not at all hampered by his cast, and I certainly hadn't expected that.

'Always was a pretty mover, Curly was,' said his mate, quietly. 'Fancy a cuppa, Doc?'

'I do,' said the doctor.

They set a special chair for me and dusted it before I sat down. I must have looked very tired because the taller one offered to put some rum in my tea. The doctor said that it mightn't be a good idea.

Presently Curly came back and they all introduced themselves. The smaller one who did the talking was called Owen and the taller one was called Bruce. They weren't afraid, they said, of the flu.

'Nah, we already had it,' said Curly. He was pale but drank his tea like the others, very black and sweet. 'No one's getting this one who had *la grippe*. But you can tell us, Doc, is it really killing people?'

The doctor told him that it was.

'Then what's the government doing about it? Strike a light, after all we've been through, this is a bit stiff.'

'You ought to know that you can't rely on governments,' said Dr Barnes, blowing on his tea.

'He's right there,' said Curly.

'So we have to look after ourselves,' said the doctor. He was planning something, I could hear it. Owen grinned at Curly.

'We're good at that, eh, mates?'

'Then what are you doing getting drunk when your neighbours are sick?' said the doctor, still in that quiet voice.

'But what can we do? We ain't sick-nurses.'

'No, you're just strong young men,' said the doctor. 'Three doors down from you is an eight-year-old girl who had to leave her father on the floor all night because she couldn't move him. And you say that there's nothing you can do. Of course not. If at least one of you doesn't go down to number seventy-three and offer that little girl some help, I'll lose all faith in the AIF. As for you,' he turned to Curly, 'keep to your bed as much as you can for a week. I'll come back tonight with something to make you sleep. I'd say no alcohol, but I know soldiers. After a week we can make you a crutch and six weeks later, God willing, you can get drunk again if you've got nothing better to do. That will be five shillings. Good day.'

Owen paid us and we left. As he helped me up onto the trap he said, 'Don't let the old doc worry. We'll fix it up bonzer.'

Then we trotted away.

By the time we came home it was almost dinner time and I had to wash and Mum sent me to rest. Mike goes along with Doctor in the evenings, as it isn't really suitable for me to go with him at night. I'm so tired and I've got such a lot to think about.

But I wish I could stop seeing that dead, blue face. I keep looking for comparisons. Like a slate floor. Like a cast iron stove. Like the bluing on the barrel of a gun.

It might be better to put 'Lord Have Mercy Upon Us' on the door. At least that would be something.

7th January

It's Tuesday. I got up early this morning and completed all of my cases notes for yesterday. I am keeping up my case notes for future reference.

Uncle Donald said he had a headache so I gave him some of the aspirin and he decided to have a bit of a lie down. Dad retreated to his old place under the lemon tree and the children joined him to play 'Sunday games', which are supposed to be quiet, so they wouldn't wake Uncle Donald.

I set out in my apron and mask with the doctor. He goes out every day. It is amazing how usual it feels. It is only a few weeks since I was so scared of Dr Barnes that I never spoke to him.

He has told me that this flu is not just an epidemic. It is a pandemic. All over the world, people are dying of it. They have it very badly in America. And in Europe. Dr Barnes's brother, who is a consultant physician to the Governor of Victoria, received a letter from his friend in Harley Street, London, asking if he had found any effective remedies and describing some experiments they are doing with prison volunteers. Most of the world is calling this flu the Plague of the Spanish Lady. We are calling it the Spanish Flu, though they think it might have come from China. And it is clear that the soldiers and others—like me—who caught *la grippe* last year are not catching this flu, so there will be some people left alive in the world even if—no, I won't finish that sentence.

We went on to the house where the dead man had been. The dead man was gone but the woman still lay in the one clean sheet I had found before. It was no longer clean. The three boys said that Mrs Benson, next door, had only stayed as long as it took for the 'men to come and take Dad'. They were hungry and dirty, as was their mother, and the baby was wailing.

This time I had some old sheets of the doctor's. He said that they were one thing that every poor household was short of and he always carried some old ones. I lit the copper and boiled the woman's bed clothes, the baby's nappies and the rags which they had all been wearing. Luckily the weather was still hot and everything was drying as I hung it out. I fed the children on soup and bread and the baby on scalded cow's milk in a bottle while the doctor moved the woman. I didn't even know her name. There was nothing in that house to tell us, almost no furniture, no papers, no books, almost no clothes. I had never been in so poor a place. The fleas hopped onto my apron in a black tide as I swept.

'Remind me,' said Dr Barnes, who had taken off his coat and was trying to knock a shaky bedstead together, using a brick as a hammer, 'to tell you about the hero Hercules and the cleansing of the Augean stables. In fact, that might be an idea. Let's move this poor woman out here,' and he carried her into the yard where the sheets were drying and laid her on the ground.

'Now we need a bucket. You there, Mrs Benson!' he bellowed over the back fence. 'Lend me a bucket?'

All we heard was the snip as the back door closed fast. Mrs Benson wasn't going to lend us anything. The doctor swore. Then he seemed to make up his mind.

'Over you go, Miss Mac,' he said, boosting me up to the fence and over it. 'Grab that bucket and that shovel. Also the yard broom. Might as well be hung for a sheep as a lamb,' he said.

I was furious with the woman. How could she hide in her house while her neighbours died? And she'd left those children. Heartless beast, I thought, and took both brooms, the bucket and a floorcloth, hanging over the fence. I handed all these things to the doctor and managed to get myself over after them.

'Fill the copper again,' he ordered. 'Then we are going to swill down the house, drown the fleas and lice, and powder everything with flea bane. After this,' he said as I did as ordered, 'I will never need to employ a housemaid again.'

It took us an hour to scour the house and I washed those children and doused them in carbolic. Then I fed them more soup to comfort them for being so clean. The woman was laid, re-clothed, in a clean bed.

But that still didn't solve the problem. Someone had to look after these children, and clearly Mrs Benson wasn't going to do it.

'What's your name?' the doctor asked the eldest boy.

'Tommy,' he said.

'And your last name?'

'Last name?' he asked.

'What did your father call you?' asked the doctor.

'That little nuisance,' said the child. Clearly he didn't know his surname.

'Did your mother have any papers? Certificates? Her marriage lines?'

'Lines?' the boy asked.

Of course. No respectable woman would lose her marriage certificate. Tommy went to the privy and pulled up a brick from the floor. He gave the doctor a leather purse.

'Dad always took her pennies for drink,' said Tommy. 'So she hid 'em.'

The purse contained seven and elevenpence ha'penny and two garnet rings. It also contained birth certificates for the children and a marriage certificate.

I began to wonder whether these children were actually going to miss their father. All of them had bruises and the scars of old injuries.

'Mrs Warrell? Can you hear me? I will find someone to look after your children. Before the day is out. I promise.'

I don't know whether she heard him. The baby was full and asleep and the children had settled down to play jack stones under the drying sheets as we brushed dead fleas off our clothes and went out to Bethesda.

When we came back to Curlew Street, where the soldiers lived, we found that a great change had come over it.

Doctor Barnes went to see Matty's mother, who he is sure will recover because she is sweating pints and already asking for food. The house had been cleaned, the invalid had been washed and changed and the sheets were boiled and hung out in the yard to dry. There was food in the kitchen, and Matty was sitting down at the kitchen table eating bread and jam with her little sisters. The man in the house wasn't her father, but the lodger, and he was dead and had already been taken away. Curly was sitting on the front porch, drinking tea, his cast stretched out in front of him, and Pat, the dog, at his side. Curly grinned at us.

'I'm just waiting for the milkman,' he explained. 'Bruce made me a bonzer crutch and I can get about all right. They're along away, at that doss house.'

'Very good,' was all the doctor said, but he was pleased.

All the people in the boarding house had been moved into the front garden. They were lying on army issue camp beds. Such an alteration! From inside the house I could hear swearing and thumping. I could smell neat lysol.

What had happened? Doctor attended to each of the patients. They had been washed. One man was complaining that he hadn't been scrubbed like that since his old mum died. A shade had been rigged to keep the sun off the patients and everyone was still alive.

Then out of the house came the little boy and the old man. The man was carrying a big pot of gruel. I always thought it tasted like wallpaper paste, but Doctor said it was very strengthening for invalids.

'What's been happening here?' asked Dr Barnes.

'Dunno,' said the old man. 'These two soldiers come down, had a look around, said "Strewth! Pongs worse than the trenches!" then they sloped off, came back with all those beds and the tent, rigged up the shade, boiled up the copper and washed everyone, carried 'em all out into the garden, and now they're working on the house. Don't reckon that they know it's the dirt that holds it together. Came up with the makings for gruel and me and the nipper here cooked it.'

A huge roll of soiled, threadbare oilcloth emerged from the house. Behind it a man wiped his brow, gave another shove, and pushed it down the steps and into the street.

Behind him a wave of water sloshed down the steps. It smelled very powerfully of disinfectant.

'G'day, Doc!' said Owen. 'That's the last rag of that rotten cloth. A man almost didn't need to shift it. The bugs was underneath crying out "heave-ho!" all the while. Now if Curly catches the milkman we'll have porridge in a tick.'

'Who is working in the house?' asked the doctor. 'You can't have done all this by yourself.'

'Oh, we called up a couple of mates. They was at a loose end, too. We was in a fever hospital in France. We know how they work. Billo and Thommo used to be medical orderlies. They took one look at the floor and said all that oilcloth had to go and so it's gone. Once the house dries out we can move these poor b— Sorry, Miss, didn't see you there. I mean to say, once the floor has dried we can move these poor blighters back inside. Shouldn't be long.'

'And where did you get an army tent and all those camp beds?' asked Dr Barnes. He was smiling.

Owen tapped the side of his nose. 'Least said, soonest mended, eh? All that stuff lying around. No one using it. The war's over now. Billo always knows where to organise a few things. Army'll never miss 'em.'

'My faith in the AIF was not wasted, Miss Mac,' said Dr Barnes and the soldier grinned. 'Good, good. Now if you can go to each house in this street and make sure everyone else is well, you will have done even better. Oh, and here is a note,' he scribbled with his fountain pen, leaning his paper on my shoulder, 'saying that you are acting under my orders and with full authority. It doesn't mean anything,' he added, waving the note in the air to dry the ink, 'but if the landlady recovers, she might be cross about her oilcloth.'

'If she recovers I was going to remind the old chook

that you can't keep people in kennels the RSPCA would go crook about. But thanks,' said Owen. From inside came the sound of crashing and splashing and a volley of indelicate language.

'Owen! Come and blanky get this blanky sofa off me!' yelled someone.

'Carry on,' said Dr Barnes. Owen saluted and went inside, calling, 'Hold your flamin' horses, I'm on me way!'

'One should never,' said Dr Barnes, 'underestimate the kindness of the common man.'

We came back to the house where Miss Jones was crying for her wedding dress. Her fever was still 105 degrees Fahrenheit and showed no signs of breaking. Her mother had cut her long hair and was laying wet sheets on her. 'It'll never be finished in time,' wailed the patient. 'And the beading, the beading isn't done.' Her fingers strayed over the breast of her white nightgown, plucking at the plain surface. 'And what will Johnny think?'

Her mother was wringing out sheets and weeping. Doctor sat down and tried to get her to swallow some water in which aspirin had been dissolved, but she said it was bitter and spat it out. He left me to try again while he spoke to the mother.

'Come along,' I said, catching one of the dry, hot hands. 'Your Johnny won't want to see you like this. And the dress will be finished.' Perhaps because I was a new voice, she seemed to hear me.

'Will it be finished?' she demanded.

'I promise,' I said firmly. 'All you have to do is drink this and sleep for a while.'

She swallowed the aspirin and made a face at the taste. I gave her some lemonade and she drank that as well.

'You promise?' she said. 'You'll see to it yourself, madame?'

I thought that it must be an expensive dress from a French dressmaker, so I thought I had better be French. 'The matter shall have my personal attention, mademoiselle,' I said. Then I racked my brains for something to say about clothes. Florence often talked about fashion but I hadn't paid any attention. 'We shall have the latest, the very latest style,' I said firmly. 'Scalloped neckline and beading in the pattern you have chosen.'

'Orange blossoms,' said the girl, and closed her eyes.

In a moment she was asleep. Her mother swept me up into a brief, fierce hug. The brooch on her dress dented my cheek.

'Good, keep her cool, get her to take more fluids, and I'll be back tonight,' said the doctor. 'Well done, Miss Mac. Now for the tent dwellers.'

The old man was sitting by a tiny, almost smokeless, fire over which a pot of soup was cooking. I could hear the young man counting. One, two, three, four. He never got past four.

'No change,' the old man said as we stooped to go into the tent. 'But the Council man came past and told me to move on. I told them I had two sick men and he said they'd have to go to hospital. They'll die there,' he said sadly. 'Everyone dies there.'

'Ridiculous!' said Dr Barnes through his mask, employing my shoulder to write another note. 'Give this to them if they come back. You are doing an excellent job. Why overload public facilities which are already overloaded? What's your name?'

'Lee,' said the old man. 'James. That's my son, Reuben, and my grandson, Faro.'

'Gypsies?' asked the doctor, writing in the names.

'Yes,' said Mr Lee flatly.

'Where are the rest of the Lees?'

'Geelong,' said Mr Lee, a little surprised, I think, that the doctor didn't say anything else about him being a gypsy. 'We came down with a string of horses. Sold 'em and were about to get on the train when Reuben got sick, and then Faro.'

'They're best left where they are and I've said that they are too sick to move. Councils! They ought to be looking after people, not oppressing them! On my way home, Miss Mac, remind me to call on the mayor.'

The only safe thing to say was 'Yes, Doctor' so I said it. Dr Barnes was very angry and the mayor had better watch out because he was going to catch it hot if he argued with the doctor in this mood. 'They're no better, but they're no worse,' he reported to Mr Lee. 'That's a good sign. Keep up the fluids.'

We went back to Bethesda, standing patiently by the side of the road.

'What's that you're saying, Miss Mac?' he asked.

'It's just a skipping rhyme,' I said, not aware that I had said it aloud.

> *My mother said*
> *I never should*
> *Play with the gypsies*
> *In the wood*

'Ha!' said the doctor. 'Harmless people, for the most part. But separate and different, and that always makes people hate them. Eh?'

'I don't know,' I replied. 'I don't hate them. I never met one before. Mum says they used to come through here selling clothes pegs and Grandma McKenzie says they steal chickens.'

'That could be said of other folk,' said Dr Barnes. I could tell that he was still angry by the way his beard bristled so I stayed silent until we came to the house with the yellow door.

Mrs Kerr was still seeing spiders and her husband was half-distracted.

'She never stops,' he said, rubbing his eyes. He had not shaved and perhaps he had not slept either.

'Go and have a wash and a shave,' said the doctor. 'We'll see to her for a while.'

'Spiders!' screamed Mrs Kerr.

'They're gone,' I said, grabbing her hands. Perhaps I could do the same for Mrs Kerr as I had for Miss Jones. 'There are no more spiders,' I suggested.

She pulled away from my grasp. 'No, no,' she moaned.

'Not going to work this time,' decided the doctor. He bade me bring the bag and filled the hypodermic syringe.

'Not morphine,' he said to me. 'Morphine is the best pain killer but it can bring on delusions in a sensitive subject.'

Mrs Kerr was certainly sensitive. Her mouth was cracked because she refused to drink and her eyes stared, red-rimmed, at the spiders that only she could see.

'What is it then? No, wait, I know that smell. It's paraldehyde.' No one could mistake it for anything else.

It smelled revolting. Dr Barnes held the syringe up to the light and tapped it to bring any bubbles to the surface.

'Yes, it had a bad effect on your father, but he was taking too much. Usually I don't give sleeping draughts in fevers, but in this case she's wearing herself out, and exhaustion kills just as well as the flu. Take her arm, turn her elbow this way.'

He gave the injection into the vein. 'You shall do the next, Miss Mac,' he said, rubbing Mrs Kerr's elbow. 'It isn't difficult. There now, Mrs Kerr, how do you feel?'

Mrs Kerr gave a gasp and sank back onto her pillow, silent for the first time in days. Her pulse was still fast, but not racing. Her temperature was only 102 degrees, a great improvement.

Then Mr Kerr appeared at the door, face covered in soap, sure that, since her voice had failed, his wife was dead.

It took us some time to reassure him and then we were out on the road again, heading for Mr and Mrs Thomas, whose mother had said that she couldn't cook or clean. Doctor had been rather rude to her and I was surprised to be allowed into the house again.

The elder Mrs Thomas showed us two spotless patients and even took me into the kitchen where a large pot of mutton soup was cooking. It smelled a little strange.

'I followed the recipe,' she said to me.

'I think you're supposed to peel the onions,' I told her. 'But it will be perfectly nourishing as it is.'

'I've never done any work,' she said, a little wistfully. 'Gels were not taught anything useful in my day. I spent yesterday finding out how much I didn't know. I have engaged a nurse for the night,' she added.

Doctor gave her another bottle of the blue mixture. She looked him in the eye. 'Have I done well?' she asked.

'Always knew you could, m'dear,' said the doctor. 'Keep up your strength now. Get the nurse to make some jelly. I'll be back,' he said.

Doctor shook the reins and we set off at a trot towards the centre of town.

'The mayor?' I asked.

He nodded, grimly. He scared me. I wondered what effect he would have on the mayor.

I have to write about Doctor and the mayor, but it will have to be tomorrow.

8th January

The Town Hall was huge. It was a stone building with pillars like trees. We drove straight in and left Bethesda with the gate keeper, whom Dr Barnes had cured of a stubborn case of the itch. He promised to feed and water her. I took off my mask and then Doctor told me to come so I ran after him in my apron and cap.

A young man tried to stop the doctor from going into the Mayor's office but he was brushed aside. I was in awe of the wood panelling and the red plush carpet, on which I was walking in shoes which reeked of carbolic. Doctor was not impressed. The Mayor was sitting in a great carved chair behind a desk as shiny and bare as a dinner table. He looked a bit startled as Dr Barnes stormed in and bashed his fist on the table.

'You must do something!' he shouted.

'I say, old fellow, calm down,' said the Mayor.

'I will not!' shouted Doctor. 'You must do something about this flu.'

'Flu? We don't have the flu, someone would have told me. There would have been an announcement,' stammered the Mayor.

'I'm making an announcement,' the doctor pointed out. 'We have an epidemic.'

'I haven't heard anything official,' said the Mayor, shrinking away.

'This is official!'

'I haven't seen anything under the Health Act. I would need authorisation. I'm responsible to the ratepayers for their money, you know.'

I thought the doctor was actually going to explode.

'Listen, you fool, we don't have one case of the flu, we've got seventy, and soon there will be hundreds. I have just come from a house where the father is dead, the mother is stricken, and there are four children who need care. What are you going to do about it?'

I was standing, rooted to the spot. I wondered if the Mayor would have the police called and the doctor arrested. The young man, his secretary, was standing beside me. Of all things, he was trying not to laugh. I could not understand it.

'I, er, I mean, you are the Public Health Officer, Dr Barnes, of course, but what can we do? It's not my business to look after lost children. They should go to the orphanage.'

'Are there no prisons? Are there no workhouses?' shouted the doctor, quoting *A Christmas Carol* by Charles Dickens, which I had read last year at school. 'If you had an ounce of brain, man, you'd realise that only firm and immediate action can avert a calamity.'

'It's that bad?' quavered the Mayor.

'Tell him, Miss Mac,' roared the doctor, and I started to tell the Mayor what I had seen. I was nervous about speaking to the mayor so boldly, but no one disobeys Doctor when he is in this mood. I was much more scared of him than of the Mayor.

The secretary had vanished while I was speaking

and came back with a stout lady in a blue dress. She smelled of ashes of roses, very sweet. She was carrying a long roll of paper and a pencil in her hand. Both men stared at her.

'My dear,' said the Mayor, 'I'm just having a consultation with Dr Barnes.'

'Dr Barnes,' said the Lady Mayoress. 'How nice to see you.'

'Madam,' said Dr Barnes, breathing fire, 'I was just telling your husband . . .'

'And I have just been trying to persuade my husband that we must do something about this flu. It is spreading very fast. I have all the church ladies available. We will need to buy some supplies, of course. Sheets, medicines, food. I am hoping that my husband will release some of the council's charitable fund.'

Doctor, who had gone an even darker red when this lady came in, let out his breath in a snort of relief. He wrote a hasty note on the list with the lady's pencil.

'Excellent. Begin with these addresses, please. The Warrell children will need immediate attention. And we must find out more quickly which households are stricken.'

'Hold on, Doctor, we can't have the council officers trespassing,' protested the Mayor. Both his wife and the doctor looked at him with the same expression.

'In deference to the presence of your able and

intelligent wife, sir, I will restrain my tongue,' said the doctor.

'All the same, we can't just kick down doors,' said the Lady Mayoress.

'What about milkmen?' I asked. Then they all looked at me. A few weeks ago I would have been afraid but now I was more sure of myself and explained. 'Well, they come every day, and they'd notice if the milk hasn't been taken in,' I said. 'Like at the Warrell house. The billy was full of sour milk and that's how we found out that they were sick.'

There was a long pause and I began to think that I had been too bold to speak in such company and that I ought to hold my tongue in front of my elders and betters, as Grandma always said. Then the Lady Mayoress laughed.

'Oh, my good and worthy Miss Mac,' said Dr Barnes. 'You'll talk to the milk company?' he asked the Mayor. He nodded. 'The list to be given to the ladies, and also to me, first thing?' The Mayor nodded again. He seemed stunned. 'And by the way, there is a man called Lee camping by the railway line. Keep your officious dog catchers away from him! He has my leave to stay there as long as he wishes. Now, madam,' he said to the stout lady, 'let us make plans. Good day, Mr Mayor,' he said.

'This way,' said the Lady Mayoress. 'Hello,' she said to me. 'My name is Mrs Collins. I think we should all have some lunch, don't you? If I know that doctor you've been slaving since early morning with never a bite.'

I never expected my career as doctor's assistant to include sitting down at a very nice cold lunch, with ham and chicken jelly and white bread, with the Lady Mayoress. Even the doctor paused long enough in his list of things which must be done right now to eat a few sandwiches and drink several cups of coffee.

Mrs Collins had one of those soft, pretty, fat faces with two chins. My mother would have said that she wore too much powder and perfume, but after the things I had been smelling lately I thought she was lovely. She had a long string of pearls which she played with as she talked and her hands were soft as petals. I couldn't imagine her scouring out a hovel and brushing fleas off her apron.

'We need to help some of the women to look after their neighbours,' she said to the doctor. 'They are working women who can't afford to take time off, even if they would want to. If not in money, then reward them in some way.'

'How good are you at getting money out of your husband?' asked the doctor, his mouth full of cucumber in vinegar.

'I have had some successes,' she said, smiling. 'Now, Doctor, I shall set about your list at once. Before you go, I would like you to write out some rules for my ladies. How is this flu nursed?'

'Carbolic masks, as we think it may be airborne. Cool drinks, soup, cold sponging to bring down fever, aspirin, orange flower water,' the doctor scribbled. 'Fresh air, constant attention. That's all,' he said, laying down the pencil.

'Nothing more?' asked Mrs Collins. 'No cure?'

'No cure,' said Doctor Barnes.

9th January

It's still hot, but Mum says that there will be a change. She's good at weather. She says it's from years and years of drying nappies.

When I came home today Mum was awake and we sat down like friends to discuss the flu. We were just swapping stories, because there still isn't a cure. All the clever doctors in the university hospitals can't find one and, as Dr Barnes would say, we must cultivate our own garden.

Since we got Mrs Quilty to come in and do the rough scrubbing as well as the washing, the house has been easier to manage. And now I'm not home as much as I was, Amelia has taken over looking after the smaller children. She's probably better at it than I was, because she just slaps both sides in a fight and tells them to behave, while I used to try to find out what had happened and who was right. Lily hates being slapped. It might tangle her hair, so she doesn't tease Albie as much and it's much quieter.

I told Mum about the soldiers meeting Mrs Collins, the Lady Mayoress. She stood at the gate of that awful boarding house and they came out to meet her and she asked them what they needed. They went all shy. Luckily Matty, who was curious, had come out of her house and picked some geraniums. She went up to Mrs Collins and gave her the flowers and she was touched.

Dr Barnes said, 'That child will be a diplomat's wife.'

The soldiers smiled at Matty, who is a general favourite.

Then Mrs Collins was shown around the house. I went too. It is terribly clean, and so were the patients. Mrs Collins told Owen that he was a fine example of a young man and she hoped her own son would grow up like him. Then she loaded them down with tinned food, sheets, spare clothes, cutlery, dishes, pots, blankets and a bottle of medicinal brandy. All this was carried in her own mayoral motor car and handed out by her own chauffeur in a grey uniform and peaked cap. Then the Lady Mayoress got in and was driven to the next address.

Owen seemed at a loss for words. Curly said, 'Strewth!'

Doctor and I then went on to see what had happened to the Warrell family. A nice lady in a gingham apron was there. The children were wearing new clothes. The littlest boy was so impressed by the brightness of his clean shirt that he kept rubbing it as though the shine hurt his eyes. The lady had them all sitting in a row in the backyard, learning to read.

'Poor tykes,' said Dr Barnes. 'They'll be washed to within an inch of their lives.'

Mrs Collins's chauffeur unloaded a camp bed, army issue, which the soldiers had donated and we at last got poor Mrs Warrell up off the floor.

I told Mum about the gypsies on the railway reserve. I said that the patients in tents seemed to do well.

'Our hospital is moving the patients out to the balconies, like the patients with tuberculosis. They all need fresh air,' agreed Mum. 'But there are so many that we haven't got a corridor left. They're opening the Town Hall and the Exhibition Buildings and they want to take over the Lyric Theatre. I don't know where this is going to end, Charlotte.'

'Neither does Dr Barnes,' I said. 'Neither do I.'

'Well, you are certainly gaining a lot of experience,' sighed Mum, looking at our identical, red, scrubbed hands. 'And this will at least tell all those nice ladies about the terrible conditions in which the poor live.

They have no idea, the Mrs Collinses of the world. I had no idea either.'

'Didn't you?' I coaxed. Mum never talks about the old days when she lived in Kew and her family owned a carriage.

'Not the faintest,' said Mum. 'I was so bored. Nothing to do all day but sew a fine seam. In fact, seams would have been too common. We only did embroidery. I wasn't very good at embroidery. I wanted to be a nurse. Oh, the rows there were! My mother weeping and my father forbidding me to leave the house. But I had my own way,' said Mum, rather sadly. 'I went out one day and signed on at the hospital, and then they couldn't get me back. Such a fuss! Then Mother got it into her head that I'd marry a doctor. They were very upset when I married a carpenter. And I'm glad they died on that yacht before they saw what became of me,' she said. 'Now, let's have some tea.'

That was strange. I know that Grandma and Grandpa didn't speak to Mum for a long time after she married Dad. They sent a silver cup for my christening, though, and one for Amelia. Then they were drowned in a boating accident. Uncle Donald is Mum's only brother. There was a lot of money, I believe, but Mum won't use any of it for us because Dad won't have it said that he married a rich woman. It's all in trust. I can't touch mine until I'm twenty-one. And when I am, I am going to medical school. I was about to ask Mum whether we could break the trust and have some of the money now, but I'm glad I didn't. Mum looked very tired. She took two aspirins with her tea and went to lie down again.

10th January

This afternoon after I had returned from the daily round with the doctor, Amelia came to me and said, 'I'm hot'. I put one hand on her forehead and told her to go straight to bed. Lily was already sitting on the side of her little bed. Her head was as hot as fire.

I had seen that sudden rise in temperature before. I went quietly into Mum's room and touched her hand.

'Mum, I think Amelia and Lily have it.' Somehow I couldn't bring myself to say the name of the disease.

'God have mercy upon us,' said Mum.

We got them into their nightgowns and into bed. We made them lemonade. Lily insisted on taking her old doll, Belinda, to bed with her. It was such a hot day that we let them lie under cool sheets.

'Is it . . .' I heard Uncle Donald ask Mum, outside the room.

She did not reply. I saw him hug her.

'We've got through some tough times, Alice. We can get through this,' he said.

For a while Amelia was talkative. She could see things and they weren't spiders.

'I can see them coming, two by two,' she said.

'Who?' I asked.

'The animals, two by two, the wombat and the kangaroo . . .'

She had always loved the Noah's Ark. I listened to her naming all the animals. That must have been a really big ark to fit them all inside.

I went next door and called to Dr Barnes. 'Don't let Florence come!' I said loudly. 'Dr Barnes! We've got it. Lily and Amelia. Can you come?'

'Instantly, Miss Mac,' he said. 'Just the two girls?'

'Yes,' I said, my heart sinking. He touched my forehead as he came down the steps. 'No warmer than the weather,' he said soothingly. 'Now don't worry,' he added. 'You didn't bring this here. It's everywhere.'

'Fine strong children,' he said later, doling out papers of aspirin and a bottle of the blue mixture. I had seen him do this hundreds of times but now it seemed that he was the only one who could save us. Amelia was still counting animals and Lily lay moaning in a restless sleep.

'The young feller all right?' he patted Albie, who seemed scared but healthy. 'And what about you, eh, Donald? Alice? Any headaches? No? Good. Keep them cool, lots of fluids,' he said, and went out to talk to Dad, who was sitting under the lemon tree as usual.

I sat down next to Amelia again. I am writing this in my diary because it gives me something to do. I am very afraid and I can't just sit here. I know how fast this flu can move. One day people are robust; the next—no, I will not speak of my fears. Lily and Amelia are strong and since Uncle Donald arrived we have been living like fighting cocks on the best of food. I won't despair. Not while Uncle Donald doesn't. He sent me to get some rest. As I went out I heard him singing Lily's favourite song.

'There's a long, long trail a-winding, into the land of my dreams . . .'

In spite of it being so hot, I slept, and when I woke Uncle Donald had made dinner. It was, he said, French hash. It tasted a bit strange, but he was so proud of it that we ate it all. Dad seemed shocked. He doesn't go out much so he didn't know how bad the flu was until Mum told him.

'They are filling every public building in Melbourne with the sick,' she said. 'They are holding up trains at the border between New South Wales and Victoria. They have troopships quarantined out in the harbour. More people have caught this flu than any population has ever done since the days of the Black Death.'

'It has an incubation period of four days,' I said. 'The first sign is a terrible headache and a high fever. Doctor Barnes lent me a thermometer. He said to take everyone's temperature.'

Mine was normal. Mum's was normal. Dad's was normal. But Uncle wouldn't let me take his temperature. When I gave it to him he dipped it in his tea.

'This tea has the flu,' he said, and shook it down. We laughed.

Mum sent word that she has to care for her own children and the hospital sent a telegram asking her to come when she could. They need her. I still have to work. Dr Barnes needs me. Uncle Donald said he'd manage the night nursing, and sent me to bed.

11th January

No change in Lily and Amelia.

When I woke, the kettle had already boiled and Uncle Donald was about to go to sleep. Mum will watch while I'm away and then it will be my turn.

I don't like the look of Lily. She hasn't said a word, and her temperature is 105 degrees. Her long hair is plaited away from her face and Mum has been bathing her all the time, but it hasn't helped so far.

This morning, very early, I heard Florence calling and I whispered to her to stay away.

'Father says that if I stand here—he's put this garden bench on the place—I can talk to you. Can you hear me?'

'Oh, Florence,' I was so glad to hear a voice which wasn't worried. 'Are you feeling well?'

'Yes, except Father hasn't let me or mother go out. Until yesterday. Mother is on the Ladies' Auxiliary. They have been delivering soup and supplies. She asked him if we could go and help and he said we could and that we owed it all to a lady called Mrs Benson. Who's Mrs Benson? I never knew a Benson, unless it was that disagreeable pimply boy at school.'

I laughed and told her about how the doctor and I had stolen Mrs Benson's bucket. It was so nice to hear her voice. She sat down on the bench and began to ask me what I had been doing. I told her a little of it. She shuddered.

'How nasty. Charlotte, how can you bear it?'

'It's interesting,' I replied. 'And we can help.'

'Father says there's no cure,' she said doubtfully.

'But not everyone will . . . if they are cared for . . . Oh, Florence, I'm so worried about Lily and Amelia.'

'Poor Charlotte! I wish I could touch you!'

'No, don't come any closer.' I was recalled to my duty. 'I had better get dressed. Your father will be here in a moment. Oh, and Florence, what is a good decoration for a wedding dress?'

'Crystals,' she said, quite sure. 'Crystal beads.'

'Thank you,' I said, and scrambled into my clothes. I heard Florence saying that she would be back tonight.

I do so want someone to talk to who isn't frightened. Even though Florence isn't frightened because she doesn't know enough to be frightened.

I went into the house and smelled the flu smell. In my own house. Wet mice.

Later

I am writing this in the girls' room. It's five o'clock. It's still very hot but Mum was right, there is a change coming. I can smell salt and that means the wind has shifted. Cool breezes come from the sea.

Today I saw the most amazing thing. Miss Jones had stopped talking about her wedding dress and was lying in a stupor. The doctor shook his head. Her face was almost as blue as a slate floor and she was dragging in each breath with tremendous effort.

Then suddenly she sat bolt upright, choked, and blood spurted from her nose. It went all over her bedclothes and her nightgown. Dark red, almost purple, venous blood. Mrs Jones seized a cloth and began to mop her up and then, from the edge of death, she smiled. It was ghastly, for her teeth were all bloody. Then she looked down at herself and began to cry.

'My wedding dress,' she wailed. 'I've got blood all over my wedding dress!'

She was better! Mrs Jones hastily stripped her and

the bed and reassured her daughter that her wedding dress was safe and that she was only wearing a common nightgown and she said sleepily, 'Why, of course. I shall have the latest.'

'Crystal beads,' I told her, and she allowed herself to be sponged and re-clothed. Her temperature was down to normal and she just seemed to be very tired.

She went to sleep, murmuring, 'Crystal beads.'

'Beef tea. Build her up. She's exhausted. You, too. She'll do,' said Doctor to Mrs Jones. 'Get some sleep.'

'Now that was very interesting,' he said to me as we jolted off towards the Lee camp. 'Have you heard of bleeding, Miss Mac?'

'No,' I said. 'I mean, not as a treatment.'

'Used to be the thing to do in cases of doubt,' he said. 'B'God, I'll try it.'

The old gypsy was sitting over his tiny fire. He was singing to himself. He had a very good, sweet voice. The tune was mournful.

The cholera's coming, oh dear, oh dear,
The cholera's coming, oh dear.
But if you but get fed,
Have a blanket and a bed,
Then you can lay down your head,
Without no fear . . .

'Hello, Mr Lee,' said Dr Barnes.

'Faro's bad,' said Mr Lee. 'But I reckon my son Reuben have turned the corner.'

Dr Barnes looked. 'Reuben is indeed, better, and if he continues on this path he will be out of danger in a couple of days. Did the council bother you again?'

'Came round and gave me a better tent, a pot, some food. Said you sent 'em. Thanks,' said Mr Lee.

'Why aren't they in it, then?'

'Two man job,' said Mr Lee. He never wasted a word.

The doctor and Mr Lee put up the new tent. I could not help noticing that it was khaki and marked 'Army Property'. Then they moved Reuben and his bed into the new tent. Faro was black faced and gasping. They both looked at him.

'There's something I could try,' said Dr Barnes. 'Is he swallowing water?'

'Aye, and soup.'

'Get me a scalpel, Miss Mac. This may not work,' he warned Mr Lee.

'No odds,' said Mr Lee. I could not see any emotion on his old, wrinkled face. 'He can't last long like this.'

Doctor bared the young man's arm and cut into the vein at the elbow. Nothing happened. He cut deeper and could not get a drop of blood. It was as if it had dried in the veins. The old man grabbed Faro, hauled him into a sitting position, and shook him, hard. It seemed so cruel.

But then blood ran out of the cut. It was thick and almost blue. Presently it ran more freely and Doctor let a lot of it spill to the ground before he put a tiny stitch in the wound and bound it up.

'Make him swallow as much water as he can hold,' he ordered. 'There! Listen! That sounded better.'

Faro began to cough, spat, coughed some more.

'Why did you shake him?' I asked Mr Lee as he and the doctor carried Faro into the new tent. It was higher; I could stand up in it.

'Blood had all settled,' he said. 'Lying too long in one place, Missy. Not good for a gypsy, being too long in one place. You're a good girl,' he told me. 'Could almost be a gypsy girl. Not afraid.'

I didn't tell him that I was always afraid. Afraid for my family. Afraid, I suppose, for the world. Is this what those soldiers fought a war for?

I said so to the doctor and he said, 'Disease knows no borders, recognises no nationalities and salutes no flag. They'll be in a bad way in Germany, I'll be bound. It's winter there. Here my Miss Mac can wash a sheet and it's dry in an hour. Imagine what it must be like getting this flu in the middle of winter.'

'How long will it last?' I asked.

'Months,' he said. 'But not forever. This is a new disease; it burns hot like a bushfire and it'll burn itself out. In the end. I wonder how the lady with the spiders is?'

Mrs Kerr had sunk into so deep a sleep that the doctor was worried. I could see that. But the husband was relieved and the doctor didn't say anything to him.

Later again

No change in either Lily or Amelia. I'm still writing and it does distract me.

The hospital which the soldiers were conducting in Curlew Street was still tidy. Two of the patients were sitting out in the garden, drinking soup. One of them was the landlady.

'Those saucy rogues of soldiers say you told them to throw away my good floorcloth,' she said to the doctor.

'So I did, madam. And had they not done so, you would even now be explaining your pest house of a dwelling to your God,' he replied. 'Count your blessings, madam. Let me see your tongue, good, and put this in your mouth if you haven't any gratitude to express.'

She seemed ashamed after that and offered to help with the nursing as soon as she felt a little better. Doctor glared at her, but he could never be really cruel to a patient. 'Wait until your temperature is normal,' he told her. 'And amend your views, if you please, on soldiers.'

She just murmured, 'Yes, Doctor'

We looked at everyone else in the house. They all seemed no worse. Several were recovering. One had the blue face and a sign I was beginning to recognise: black feet. The blood carries oxygen, and this blood wasn't carrying any. Doctor tried bleeding him but he could not get any blood. He told Owen that he might have to call the undertaker soon.

'Not too good, eh?' said Owen. 'Heard from the corpse merchant that he's run out of coffins. So you'd better not die,' he told the patient.

We continued on our rounds.

Matty was well. Curly was sitting with the recovering mother, resting his cast on a kitchen chair. She was leaning against the bed head and smiling at something he said. The children were festooned all over him.

'Reckon you'll be better by the time I get this cast off,' Curly was saying. 'Then we can go dancing.'

Doctor chuckled about this all the way to the shining clean Warrell household, but he wouldn't tell me what he was laughing about. Mrs Warrell seemed much the same. The lady who cared for the children said that she had roused, once or twice, when the baby cried.

At the Thomas house, Mr Thomas was sane and talking. His wife was still very sick. But old Mrs Thomas was delighted and was searching through her cookery book, looking for invalid recipes.

'If she doesn't poison them with her cookery, Miss Mac, they'll pull through all right. At least, Mr Thomas will. Now, we're going home. Mrs Reilly has made you a hamper. Keep up your heart,' he said to me, just as he did to his other patients.

I took the hamper and went inside, not needing now to wash myself in carbolic, for the invader had already arrived.

Dad was sitting on the veranda. 'Just came out for a breath of air,' he said. 'It's as hot as fire inside. Lemonade in the ice-box,' he told me.

I had a thought. 'Dad, do you know how to rig a tent?'

'Yes,' he said. 'I've rigged hundreds.'

'Could we put one up, do you think, here in the yard? Move them outside where it isn't so stuffy?'

'Why don't you ask your Uncle Donald?' he said nastily.

'Because I'm asking you,' I said. I was too tired to get angry. Dad didn't reply. I went inside and sat down between Lily and Amelia. Amelia was still talking, but softer and now she didn't make sense. Mum went to rest.

12th January

It is so hot that sweat drips off my nose and down my neck and soaks my thin shirt. I have a bamboo fan and I wave it, trying to stir the air and keep off flies. There seem to be thousands of flies. Lily hasn't moved. She looks like a statue. She's always been the one with the good looks which Dad says come from Mum's side of the family. She has the golden hair and the blue eyes. Now her face is darkened and she breathes like someone tearing brown paper.

Uncle Donald brings a fresh jug of water. I tell him about the tent and he agrees it is a good idea. He looks very tired. We are all very tired. He lies down on the bed that used to be mine and says he'll just close his eyes. I wish I could close mine.

On and on, the day wears, as long as years. At five o'clock Uncle Donald goes out, saying he has to see a man about a dog. Amelia murmurs and takes water. Lily doesn't move at all.

At six Doctor Barnes comes in. He looks at Amelia and then at Lily. I know that look. But it couldn't be. She is going to get better. He manages to coax her into drinking some aspirin and quinine and goes away again.

At seven Uncle Donald comes back with two friends, carrying a huge roll of canvas. They manage to get it into the house with much toing and froing, like a lot of ants trying to move a big grasshopper. It is the tent and it has a mosquito net, Uncle says. Then we unpack some of the hamper. It has a lot of cold sausages and cold salad and it is very welcome.

The night seems to have got hotter. Dad sits out on the porch until the mosquitoes drive him inside. Mum and Uncle Donald chat for a while, trying to find something else to talk about than the flu.

I sit with the patients while they get hotter and I get hotter. Mum says she'll come at midnight.

But I'm worried now. I'm very worried.

13th January

It happened before midnight. I was washing Amelia's face when I heard Lily drag in a great breath, cough, and then stop. She didn't draw another breath.

I ran to her and shook her. She gave a rattling sigh, but she never breathed again. She was still as hot as fire but she had no pulse.

I went and got Mum. She came like a sleepwalker. She examined Lily, bringing the candle close to lift her eyelids, listen for a breath, count her pulse. There was no response. Mum sat quite still for a moment.

Then she gave a soft groan and lay down on the bed, next to Lily. I thought she was crying. I ran and banged on Uncle Donald's door. He came in his nightshirt, leaning on the dressing table.

'Lily,' I said. I couldn't say anything else.

'Go and wake your father,' he said to me, in a voice quite unlike Uncle Donald. And he wasn't going to comfort Mum. He was sitting down on his bed again.

I flew into Dad's room and pulled at his arm, making him get out of bed. 'It's Lily. And Mum. And Uncle Donald,' I gabbled.

When he came into Uncle Donald's room, Uncle Donald held out his hand and Dad took it.

'You'll have to get that tent up, Alec,' he said, and collapsed. Dad helped him into his bed and Uncle Donald passed out as his head hit the pillow.

Dad left him there and went into the girl's room. Mum would not let go of Lily, though he tried to pull her away. I was in despair. Now we were all sick, and no one but me and Dad to nurse us, and what good was Dad?

And Lily was dead. I could not realise it. She was still limp and warm but she was gone. Lily who was so vain, Lily who liked sad songs. Lily who still wore those silly pearl beads around her neck.

'Charlotte, I'd better go and call for Dr Barnes,' said Dad. 'Is Albie all right?'

'Tell him that Lily is dead,' I said. My voice didn't

even quiver. 'And Uncle Donald has it. I'll see to Albie.'

He was fast asleep and not even hot. I didn't wake him. Instead I lit the lamp and began to sponge Uncle Donald's forehead. It burned my hand, just like all the others had done. Then I went back to Amelia. Mum hadn't moved. What if they were both . . .

I knew I couldn't cry. There were too many things to do. The doctor would be coming. I tidied Amelia, put some more lavender water on a cloth and laid it on her forehead, then did the same for Uncle Donald. He was too heavy for me to move. I stripped back the blankets from his bed, though, and left just the sheet. I even opened the window, in case there was any fresh air outside.

Doctor Barnes came. He gently pulled Mum away. I put Lily's doll, Belinda, in her arms. Then Doctor Barnes and I tied up Lily's jaw in a clean bandage, just as I had done to other dead people, and wound a sheet around her. Then we carried her out to the parlour and laid her on the floor.

Then I wept and couldn't stop. The doctor left me there and went into the other room. I was so grateful to him.

14th January

It's Tuesday. I can't bear it, though, of course, I shall have to. I went out to talk to Florence. I told her about Lily and she said she'd send us some flowers. No one goes to funerals these days. There are too many of them. They go past our street all day. But Lily loved white peonies and Florence says she shall have them. She was so sweet to me. I felt a little better and was standing on the step after Florence had gone in. I heard Mum speaking to Dad.

'I worked very hard for you, Alec. I bore all your ill-temper and your envy. Then when you went away to war I raised your children alone. It was hard. You have never thanked me, or noticed how hard I worked, and Charlotte worked. Then when you came home, I didn't have a husband. I had another child. I cared for you as well. I bore with your ill temper again, your envy, your malice. Now my own little Lily is dead. And that is enough, Alec. I give up. Whether we live or die is up to you.'

Then I heard a thud as she fell forward onto Lily's bed.

Well, that's all of us. And if there's only me left, that might be the end of us.

15th January

Because he shows no sign of the flu, Mrs Barnes has been allowed to take Albie next door. Mrs Reilly always liked him and he's a good boy. And I miss him, but he'd be dreadfully in the way here. Everyone is sick. But I'm coping. I was all right until I remembered Lily reading the Book of Job and had to go and bathe Uncle Donald's forehead again so Dad didn't see me cry.

Dad is different. Now we are all sick, except me, he's changed. Even his voice has changed. It's stronger and louder.

Doctor Barnes comes night and morning. I don't know how he manages without me. He brought Owen and Bruce over to help Dad rig the tent and they turned out to have known each other in France. Owen said, 'I thought they put you in the giggle-house, old man,' and Dad said in quite a different voice, 'They did, but I escaped.' They laughed and then it was a lot of 'to you—no, that way' and 'Mind the chookhouse!' until they got the big tent up. It has the lemon tree inside it and mosquito netting all around.

The soldiers carried Mum, Amelia and Uncle Donald out into the yard and laid them on army cots which Billo 'picked up somewhere' and then they left, promising to come back for a beer. Amelia is, I think, getting better but

Mum hardly moves and Uncle Donald is delirious.

Oh Lily, oh, my own little sister.

17th January

I was in the kitchen yesterday when Dad came in. He sat down at the kitchen table and asked, 'Charlotte, how hard do you work?'

I told him, 'Like anyone.'

'Tell me what you did each day,' he said. 'When you were still at school.'

So I told him what I did every day. I choked when I came to putting everyone to bed because I had a sudden clear flash of Lily combing her hair. He patted my shoulder.

'I never knew,' he said.

I went and had a quick wash. It's so hot that I am only wearing an old cotton dress. When I came back Dad and I went out to see what we could do with the invalids.

All day we sponged and soothed, and towards dark first Dad, then I, knocked off to have a sandwich and a cup of tea. I wasn't hungry. I feel as though all my grief is on the surface of my skin, biting into me like acid. Sable came to sleep with me last night and I was so pleased to see him, even though he is furry and hot. I mustn't give way. Mum lies as though she had been stunned but Amelia is still talking, a funny little babble of nonsense.

The sky grew heavier and hotter, sultry. The clouds were so close that they were just over my head and the steamy heat beat up from the ground. I took two aspirin for my headache. I always get a headache when it is going to storm.

'Dad,' I said, 'will this tent stand a storm?'

'Ought to,' he said. 'You get your head down, Charlie. I'll watch for a bit.'

He hadn't called me Charlie since he came back from the war. I felt so uncomfortable that I did as he said and lay down on my own bed. The heat beat me down and I slept heavily.

I was woken by a crash and a scream. Thunder! Oh, Lord, I thought, and Dad has shell shock. Remember cracker night.

I ran into the garden. It was as dark as the inside of a mine and the thunder was crashing like someone dropping wardrobes right over our heads.

I couldn't see who was screaming. I felt my way into the house and found a candle, then lit the big kitchen lamp. There was shouting and crashing outside and the first drops of rain were falling. What was I going to do with Dad?

And I confess I felt angry with him, even though it

isn't his fault. He can't help it. But I took the lamp out into the yard and into the tent as a struggling body went past me and crashed to the ground. There was a blur of arms and legs. I put the lamp out of harm's way and dived onto the struggling mass, and found that the man who was screaming that awful scream was Uncle Donald, and Dad was pinning him to the ground.

'They're sending us over the top!' yelled Uncle Donald. I was sitting on his legs and Dad was sitting on his chest but he was so strong that he almost threw us off.

Dad's face was greasy with sweat and he stank of fear. But he gritted his teeth as the dreadful noise broke over us again and then, in the little calm, he said in a crisp, almost English voice, 'Stand easy, soldier! Order rescinded. Sortie cancelled. Stand down!'

Uncle Donald stopped fighting us and we managed to get him back into bed. Dad sat on him while I fetched a clothesline and we lashed him to his place. He was weeping and babbling and Dad was shaking.

'We're a pair,' said Dad. 'Better get some extra line, Charlie, in case you have to tackle me as well.'

'I won't have to tackle you,' I said, suddenly so proud of him that I could have cried. 'You're strong enough to fight it. And I'm here,' I said.

We sat down on the tent floor. I remember Florence telling me that the thunder was the Norse God Thor, driving his chariot over the sky. I told Dad and he said,

'Perishing rough road, then. Listen to the wheels crash over the cobbles! You'd think they'd lay down some duckboards in Heaven.' His voice was trembling.

Uncle Donald said, quite clearly, 'The big guns are limbering up. That was a sighting shot.'

'We're behind the lines, mate,' said Dad. 'Far behind the lines. We're almost back at Headquarters!'

Then came a flash which bleached the night. There was a huge crash. Then the rain fell like a river, straight down. It beat on the taut canvas like a drum.

'I see what you mean about the tent,' I said.

'It's a good tent, Charlie,' Dad shouted back. 'Army issue!'

I went to have a look at Amelia. She had stopped talking. Her face was still hot. I could not hear her breathing but her pulse was there, light and fast. Mum was unconscious or sleeping. I bathed their faces and got Amelia to drink some boiled water.

When I came back Uncle Donald was talking.

'This is a bad one,' he was saying. 'They'll drown in them low lying trenches. Get them into the church!' he called to someone I could not see. 'There's a stone floor in there. Stretcher bearers! Stretcher bearers!'

'Bloody war,' groaned Dad. 'Will we ever be free of it? Sorry, Charlie. Shouldn't swear in front of a lady. You're a good girl. Sit down here, then, and you can hold Don's hand, and I'll hold yours. In times like this,' said

Dad—and unbelievably, he grinned. I swear that he actually grinned. I saw his teeth flash in the half light—'we all need a hand to hold.'

So we sat in the dimness with the rain falling like stair rods and held hands. The thunder crashed and each time it did, Dad flinched and Uncle Donald yelled, 'Creeping barrage! Take cover!' and I jumped.

Presently I felt very sleepy. I leaned against Dad and closed my eyes. I didn't fall asleep because at any moment Dad might need my help but it was the first time since the flu began that I felt comforted. He was putting forth a tremendous effort not to lose control. I could feel it in his shoulders, as tense as wire.

Finally the thunder rumbled itself away to the south and the rain eased. The flame from the lamp stood up yellow and clear.

18th January

What happened after that? It's Saturday and I'm sitting in the yard writing, with the book on my knee. What happened after Dad was so brave?

We looked down at ourselves. We were all wet. In fact, we were soaked.

The yard drained towards the middle and we were

sitting in three inches of water. I hadn't noticed because I was so hot. Now it began to get cooler.

Dad got up and hauled me to my feet.

'At least it ain't mud,' he said. 'I've had enough of mud. Well, that cleared the air, didn't it? Never mind about the water,' he told me. 'It'll drain. Ground's so hard that it'll take a while to soak in, that's all. Well, the drought's broken, and this tent's held up bonzer. Let's make a cuppa. At least them blanky flies have gone. And the mozzies.'

He was right. The clouds cleared and the air cooled and all the insects had gone. Dad drank three cups of tea loaded with sugar and said he'd lie down on the veranda.

I sat in the cooling tent. I noticed that Mum had started to shiver so I hauled out blankets and wrapped everyone. Then I hung my dress over the line to dry and put on a clean one. It was an old calico dress which felt very cool and soft on my skin.

Then I heard Florence calling. I climbed up on the fence. She was standing on the garden bench.

'I just came to see if you were all right!' she called in a carrying whisper.

'Yes,' I said. For some reason I felt sure that we were. 'Bit wet. But Dad came through all right. Did your father send you?'

'Yes. I'll go back and tell him to go back to sleep. He was worried about . . . the noise.'

'Tell him to sleep,' I said. 'Florence, where did you get the story about Thor and the chariot?'

'I'll bring you the book tomorrow,' she promised. 'Your little brother slept through it all.'

Dawn was not far off. Amelia stirred. I gave her some water and aspirin. She drank it. Mum seemed to be asleep. Uncle Donald was awake.

'Hello, Charlotte,' he said. His lip cracked as he tried to smile and I dabbed at it. He drank some water and some of the blue mixture. 'Orange blossoms,' he said.

Then he closed his eyes.

The flu is cruel. Uncle Donald had always been so strong. Now he was as weak as a kitten. I don't know why people say that; kittens are very spry. Weak as a fish out of water. Limp. All the spark had gone out of his face. He was all bones, nose and forehead and chin.

So was Mum. She scared me. She didn't even make an effort to swallow. She just let the water run out of the corner of her mouth.

I went back to my chair in the middle of the tent. Dad was right. The water was draining away to feed the grass. The air was cool. I trussed up the side of the tent, facing the breeze which began to blow just as dawn greyed the sky. Dad had fought off an attack, Uncle Donald was quiet, the others were sleeping and we had survived the night.

19th January

Doctor Barnes came in with more news. The Town Hall is full of flu patients. The government have closed all the cinemas, pubs, theatres, race tracks and music halls. Doctor doesn't know if this will make a difference. I made him drink some coffee.

About coffee. Now there are no longer any deliveries Dad went down to the grocer's shop himself. You have to hand in your list and the grocer puts the bags on the floor, a safe distance away. You put the money in a dish of carbolic on the floor. We didn't have to do this because we have an account. Jimmy, the grocer's boy, is down, and so is Mrs Johnson, the grocer's wife. The shops are running out of things because trains are delayed at the border and the countryside is stricken. Dad went to the shop, as I said, and found that there wasn't any more tea, so he bought coffee. He makes it in a billy, which he swings around to settle the grounds. It's a very decided taste and I'm not sure if I like it, even with a lot of milk and sugar, but it's very good at keeping me awake.

Doctor drinks his coffee black and very strong. He says that the Ladies' Auxiliary and the Lady Mayoress have taken over the cleaning and most of the nursing. 'The ladies are getting an education into the conditions of the poor,' he said thoughtfully. 'May have a good effect once this is over. Nothing like a personal encounter with fleas and filth to make you value cleanliness.' That is true enough.

Doctor looked at Amelia and said she was recovering but he was concerned over Uncle Donald and Mum.

'Her constitution was greatly tried before she fell ill,' he said, shaking down the thermometer. 'And four years of war don't leave a lot left over to fight the flu. But while there's life there's hope, Miss Mac.'

'What happened to Mr Lee's son and grandson, Doctor?' I asked as I escorted him to the door.

'Both on the mend,' he said. 'So are the Thomases, the Warrells and the people in the boarding house, except for the one who died last night. Miss Jones is planning her wedding again. But I don't hold out much hope for Mrs Kerr. Still, we aren't dead yet. Your father is bearing up, Charlotte.'

'He's very brave,' I said. And I meant it.

21st January

I really haven't anything to write. Each day is the same, each night is the same. Uncle Donald is still delirious on occasions, and Dad calms him down. We don't need to tie him now he's weaker and can't get out of bed. Every morning we wash the patients and change their beds, we light the copper and wash the fouled sheets and hang them out. Then Dad sleeps and I watch.

Amelia is definitely better than she was. She's sitting up, starting to eat, and demanding her sewing things. Doctor saw that she wanted occupation and brought her a great basket of cloth. It's just straight seams with a frill around the neck and she can make them very fast, especially the little ones.

She's sewing shrouds. Somehow that doesn't seem strange to me, or to Amelia. She wants something to do and she's always been a very good seamstress, and we can't send them naked into the earth, can we?

22nd January

Today Uncle Donald sat up for about half an hour and ate some of Dad's onion soup. Amelia ate some too, and actually got out of bed and walked around. She's still very weak but Doctor is very pleased with her and says she can go back to her own bed if she likes.

But she doesn't want to because all of Lily's things are there. I haven't told Amelia that Lily is gone, but she knows.

So today I took a packing case from Uncle Donald's

room and collected up everything belonging to Lily. Her clothes—always better kept than ours—her doll Jeanne, her mirror, her silver vase that belonged to Grandma in which she always had flowers, summer or winter. Her little shoes. Her Bible. Her picture of 'My First Sermon' which she always thought looked like her. I was crying so much as I did this that Dad heard me.

'I'll do it,' he said.

'No,' I told him. 'It's done. That's all of her things.'

It wasn't much, for all of her short life. Dad hammered the lid on and stored the box in his own room. Then he dismantled Lily's bed and put the pieces under Amelia's bed and I went and fetched Amelia.

'It's all right,' Dad said to her. 'She wouldn't mind you having the room. Come along, daughter.'

Amelia went so far as to come into the room and sit down on the bed. Then she started to cry and I waved at Dad to go away.

'I didn't like her,' said Amelia. 'Most of the time. She was vain and silly and she used to tease Albie.'

'Yes,' I agreed. 'But she's in Heaven and she forgives us.'

'Yes,' said Amelia. 'Lily would like forgiving us,' then she cried and I cried some more. But luckily Amelia was too weak to cry for long. I tucked her up in her own bed and when I looked in on her later she was sitting up and sewing. She sews beautifully. Florence had sent the book, so I sat with her and read her the story about the bet with Loki, and Thor trying to drink the sea.

The glazed white cotton ran out from under Amelia's clever fingers. She tied off a knot and I folded the finished shroud.

'I wonder how many they will need?' she asked.

'I don't know,' I said. 'As many as you can make, perhaps.'

She lay back for a little sleep.

Uncle Donald was awake, coughing terribly. We propped him up. His face was dark but not yet blue. I sneaked a look at his feet, and they weren't black. Doctor had given him a bottle of the brown medicine. He was taking it and complaining. I liked hearing him complain.

'You know, Charlotte,' he said, after he had swallowed it and the lump of sugar which followed, 'I reckon that's straight creosote. You could paint a fence with it.'

'That's what it smells like,' I agreed.

He is coughing up clear, frothy fluid. Doctor told me to tell him immediately if it turned yellow, which would mean pneumonia. So far it is clear. Uncle Donald says that his joints don't ache any more but his chest does, which is because of all the coughing.

Mum is still fevered, restless and very sick. Dad sits by her all the time he isn't needed for the others. He holds her hand when she will let him. Dr Barnes is concerned about Mum. I can tell.

24th January

With Amelia better I have more chances to talk with Florence. Today she brought Albie to the garden bench so he could see me and I could see him. He seemed sturdy and happy enough, though he cried for Mum. I explained that he couldn't come to her yet but he is too little to understand. Mrs Reilly is upset because two of her sons have the flu. They're in her quarters at the doctor's house.

'This seems to have been going on forever,' said Florence. 'I've got a hamper and a new book. I'll put them on the front porch. You know that school isn't going back? They've closed all the schools until the flu is over.'

I didn't tell her that I wasn't going back to school anyway. To think I used to be so worried about not going to school!

25th January

Uncle Donald got up today. He walked to the veranda, bent over like an old man, holding his chest and coughing. But he got up. He was so proud of himself. He sat there for a whole hour. He says he has to get better in pure self defence, because otherwise he'll have to drink more of Dad's onion soup.

Dad's onion soup is actually Great Great Grandma McKenzie's onion soup. 'Cures all ills in man and beast,' says Dad. 'That's what my mum says.'

Dad had to get out the bicycle and ride to the Maribyrnong market gardens to get the ingredients. Dad? Riding a bike? I never would have thought it possible a few months ago. He had to put patches on the tyres and oil it because it hadn't been used for so long. Even then he had a puncture on the way home.

The future might need this soup. It certainly will if the flu comes back. So I'll write it down.

To make this soup, you peel and crush twelve bulbs of garlic into butter. Garlic is a strange little bulb a bit like a crocus, and has a terrible smell. Then you fill the pot with as many sliced onions as it will hold, sprinkle sugar on top and stir until it goes golden, then fill it up with chicken stock. It's cooked when the onions are transparent. After the first shock, I liked the taste. Amelia adores it. Uncle Donald says it reminds him of France, and he doesn't want to be reminded of France, thank you very much. He also says that we'll never catch the flu because no one will ever come close enough to breathe on us. We stink of garlic. It comes out through the skin when we sweat.

Mum won't drink it at all. In fact, she won't drink anything. A friend of hers from the hospital, Sister Patience, came to see her today and managed to convince her to drink some lemonade. She says things are bad. She's very tired.

'They're sending interstate for more coffins,' she told me. 'So you're Charlotte. Your mum is so proud of you. Have you been nursing your family on your own?'

'Me and Dad,' I said. Sister Patience looked at Dad with a curious expression but she didn't say anything, just patted me and told me I was a good girl. Then she asked about the smell and I said it was garlic.

'Funny. We've had a few Italians through the hospital and they smelled the same. Maybe it works. Can't hurt,' said Sister Patience. 'Come along, Alice, old girl, make an effort.'

Mum roused enough to drink some of the blue mixture and then closed her eyes again.

'How long has she been like this?' Sister Patience asked me.

'Ever since she got it,' I answered. 'Amelia's over it and Uncle Donald's recovering but Mum just lies there.'

'Why don't you walk me to the door?' she asked, and I did so. Just outside the gate, where no one could hear, she said very quickly, 'Listen, Charlotte, I've seen a lot of people in your mother's state. You have to rouse her. You have to make her want to live. She always said you were a clever girl. You'll have to think of something. I'll come back as soon as I can.'

Then she was gone.

What am I going to do?

28th January

Still very hot, but it's a clear heat, not that awful humidity.

Uncle Donald gets up every morning now and puts on his clothes for a few hours, before he goes back to bed in his own room. He's been very helpful with Amelia, reading to her while she sews. He's still coughing but not as badly.

Mum's still in the yard. Dad has made the tent into a Coolgardie safe. He's put buckets of water beneath each mosquito net. The water seeps up the net and the air blows through it, making a cool breeze.

Mum just lies there. Dad holds her hand and talks to her. I can hear him now, as I'm writing. 'I'm sorry,' he says. 'I let you down; I let the others down. I was too proud to take money from your family. It didn't matter what the blokes said. They're always saying things. What would they know? And they would have knocked it off if I'd told 'em I didn't care what they thought. I let you work yourself to a rag,' he said, so sadly that I have to wipe my eyes, 'while I sat here in my slippers and whinged.'

Mum doesn't hear him. Sister Patience said I had to rouse her, make her want to live. But she was so tired and then Lily was taken and she just collapsed. And now she's slipping away.

She's always been so strong that I can't believe she's just lying there like that. I'm expecting her to open her eyes and say 'Charlotte! Put the kettle on!'

Doctor Barnes came in. He was chuckling. Apparently the soldiers had got tired of being good and had tried out the Mayoress's bottle of medicinal brandy last night, and then the bottle of medicinal rum, and quite a few bottles of home-made medicinal beer. Today they were all sick and the doctor had treated them with bottles of the green stomach mixture and some medicinal aspirin.

'Too much virtue in a soldier is dangerous,' he said. 'I thought they might be sickening themselves, but no. Everyone else is recovering. How is your mother, Miss Mac?'

I told him what Sister Patience had said and he rubbed his beard.

'Yes, there must be an effort,' he said. 'But we can't induce it. She has to do it herself. She is very sick, I'm afraid. And how is my seamstress today?' he asked Amelia. Her temperature was normal and she was sewing fast. Uncle Donald was also normal, though still coughing and very weak.

'This is a bonzer book,' he said. 'Lots of good stories in it. Those Vikings were a tough lot, but. How's Alice, Doc?'

'Not too well,' said the doctor. He drew Uncle Donald outside and spoke to him in a whisper. Then he went out to see Mum. I dragged Uncle Donald into his room.

'What did he say?' I demanded.

'She's sinking,' said Uncle Donald, looking stricken. 'I've got to sit down, Charlotte. Not as strong on my pins as I used to be. What are we going to do? If she won't rouse for me, or for Alec— and hasn't he been a brick?— then for who or what?'

There's the question. I can't imagine.

Florence brought me another book, *The Heroes*, by Charles Kingsley. I had told her not to bring fairy books because I didn't think Uncle Donald would enjoy reading fairy stories. And Lily always loved them and that would make Amelia sad. I told Florence what the doctor said and she couldn't think of anything either.

Mum's not getting any worse; she's just not getting any better. Uncle Donald can get her to swallow medicine and even Dad's onion soup, but her temperature remains high. She used to be a plump woman. Now all her flesh has fallen away. Her fingers are like claws. Dad is bearing up but I know that he'll never forgive himself if Mum . . . No. I will think of something.

1st February

I don't even know what day it is. This morning Mrs Quilty came to do the washing so it must be Saturday. We got through it all with Uncle Donald and Amelia helping as much as they could. Mrs Quilty wore a mask and we couldn't really talk much. She says that her family have all had the flu except herself and she's worn to a shred. She says she couldn't go on if it weren't for her children. She says her old man is grousing that the Government shut the pubs. So he must be feeling better. Uncle Donald gave her a bottle of beer to comfort him.

I had a thought. I got Dad to make some coffee and then I let it cool. It keeps me awake, so maybe it might wake Mum. I put a lot of sugar in it. Then Uncle Donald, who is patient, sat by Mum and dripped a whole cupful gradually into her mouth. She swallowed it. She seemed to wake a little then, opened her eyes and looked around. She said hello to Dad and squeezed his hand. Then she floated off.

Then I heard Florence calling. She had Albie with her and I had an inspiration.

I held out my arms to my little brother and he raced across the forbidden ground. I hauled him up and over the fence and set him down. He belted across to Mum and threw himself on her, crying like a fountain and pounding her with his little fists. Dad went to take him away and I said, 'No, leave him.' Albie shrieked 'Mum! Mum! Mum!' like a train whistle and Mum woke and hugged him.

She opened her eyes and hauled herself up on one elbow and said, 'There, there, Mummy's here,' to Albie. Then she sneezed. Dad helped her to sit up with her back against his chest. She blinked, coughed, and then, just when she was about to float off again, Albie crawled up into her lap. He always digs in his sharp little elbows and knees when he climbs into your lap. Mum winced and Uncle Donald lifted Albie and sat him across her lap.

'Mum?' I asked.

'I can taste coffee,' she said. 'Alec? Did you make coffee?'

'Yes, love,' said Dad gently.

'Can I have some? And then I might have a little sleep. What am I doing in the yard? Charlotte?'

'Here, Mum,' I said. I was shaking.

'Is Amelia? . . .'

'Amelia's sitting up in bed and sewing,' I said. 'I'll get the coffee.'

Before I did that I ran to the fence where Florence was standing, watching.

'You're too close,' I said.

'We've got it too,' she told me. 'Mum and Mrs

Reilly. Dad's sent for nurses. You'll have to tell me what to do, Charlotte. I'm so scared.'

'Go back into the house,' I said. 'I'll come soon. Put everyone to bed, sponge their faces and hands with lavender water, and give them water. How are Mrs Reilly's sons?'

'Both over the worst, Father says. And Mike has had the flu.'

'How do you feel?' I asked. I felt her forehead. It wasn't hot. I told her I would be there directly, and ran inside to make coffee.

Mum drank the coffee and ate a whole bowl of onion soup, then fell asleep. Dad and Uncle Donald sat on the back veranda, beaming at each other.

I felt as if a great weight had been lifted off my shoulders. I felt light. Dad hugged me and Uncle Donald kissed me.

'There's a clever girl,' said Dad.

'There's a brilliant little fairy,' said Uncle Donald.

I gave him the new book and said that I had to go over to Florence's. They both looked grave at the news.

Albie refuses to leave Mum. If she has to be moved or changed he clings like a limpet and Uncle Donald has to walk him through the house until he can come back and grab her again. She's weepy and weak but she's getting better. I could dance with joy.

2nd February

Poor Florence is shattered. I think she felt that because she was in the doctor's household they wouldn't catch it. Mrs Reilly was in a high fever but it broke in a shower of sweat while I watched tonight. Once we had got her changed she went to sleep immediately. Both her sons are with her and, as Uncle Donald said long ago, for hygiene you really need a sailor. Mrs Barnes isn't so good. Dr Barnes tries not to show it, but he's very worried about her.

'It's a delicate constitution, Miss Mac,' he said. 'I don't like to leave her.'

'I can do the night calls,' I said. He rubbed his beard.

'A young girl alone at night?' he asked. 'What will you do if someone approaches you?'

'I'll cough,' I said, and he laughed.

So tonight I set out in the pony cart with Bethesda and the list. Bethesda doesn't need to be driven. She knows where all the patients are and she stops there by herself.

First was Mr Lee. He was looking almost cheerful. He introduced his son, Reuben, who was out of bed and Faro, his grandson. He was still lying down and very weak.

'I knew he was on the mend,' said Mr Lee, 'when he went past four. We had eleven horses in that string. That's what he was counting.'

I gave him another bottle of the blue mixture. Then I

smelled a really interesting smell. It was the essence of all green scents. It was rising from a tea pot.

Mr Lee said it was tea made of herbs, and he gave me a bunch. 'Rosemary for strength of heart,' he said solemnly, 'hyssop for cleansing, mint for cooling, lemon balm for soothing. Give me your hand,' he said to me.

It was strange to be sitting in a tent in the dark with a lot of unrelated men, but I was not afraid. I gave him my hand and he examined the palm.

'Great sorrow and loss. Brave,' he said, tracing a line. 'Very clever. Will get what you want,' he said. 'In time, Missy, will get all you want. You mark my words. There's the star of destiny, plain as plain. You will be,' said Mr Lee, returning my hand, 'what you want to be.'

'Thank you,' I said. I nodded to the patients, and went back to Bethesda.

I thought about that all the way to Curlew Street. What did I want to be? I wanted to be a doctor. I wanted to find a cure for diseases like this, which robbed the poor of the only thing they owned, life itself. And Mr Lee had said that I would be what I wanted to be.

Well, I intended to be a doctor. One day this would be my pony cart, my horse, my list of patients.

I had it all settled by the time I dismounted at the boarding house.

Everyone in Curlew Street was asleep except for Curly, who was siting on the front porch with a tall man.

'A sheila!' said the man, grabbing for my arm. I was affronted, and so was Curly. He swung his crutch around and stood up.

'She's not a sheila, you blank of a blanky blank,' he snarled. 'She's a nurse, and if you don't let go of her I'll blanking break your blank arm.'

'Sorry, Miss,' stammered the man—one of our patients, I saw. 'Meant no offence, Miss.'

'None taken,' I said, one of Mum's phrases. 'The doctor's wife is sick so I've come on my own.'

'Poor old Doc!' said Curly. 'We're all right here, Miss Mac. No one's died since this morning. Billo's sitting up with them,' he said.

The boarding house was clean now. I looked in at every room and found Billo at the bedside of a young man.

'He's come through,' he said, indicating a pile of wet sheets by the door. 'Sweating a treat. Reckon he'll last now. Got some more of the blue stuff? Good-o.'

When I got to the Thomas's, Mrs Thomas was sitting up and drinking some of her mother-in-law's peculiar soup.

At the Warrell's, Mrs Warrell was not only awake but sewing a new shirt for her baby from some calico which the charitable ladies had given her.

The next patient, Mrs Kerr, was, as the doctor had feared, sinking. She wasn't even worried about spiders any more. She looked like Mum had. Limp and almost lifeless.

I told her husband that I would be back in the morning. He was terribly worried.

'You have to rouse her,' I said. 'Is there anything she really, really hates?'

'She doesn't like cayenne pepper, and she can't stand Caruso,' he said. 'She said he sounds like singing treacle.'

'Well, bring in the phonograph,' I said. 'And play the Caruso record. If she won't rouse for things she likes, like flowers and perfumes and Earl Grey tea' (all of which we had tried and got no response) 'then maybe she'll rouse for something she hates. And try her with a sniff of cayenne.'

I went back to Bethesda. The doctor was right. A lot of medicine depended on faith. We trotted home again. It was black dark. Once a man spoke to me, but then he saw my apron and cap and hurried away, covering his mouth. There were a lot of children on the street. School hadn't gone back and they were running wild. Doctor had a jar of coltsfoot lollies which he always handed out, as a preventative of the flu, and I gave them some when they gathered around.

Then Bethesda took me home. I gave her to Mike, unpacked the cart and went into the house, which was very silent.

Mrs Reilly was asleep. Mrs Barnes was still in a high fever. I steeped the herbs in a tea pot and brought them in.

'Smells nice,' said Doctor. 'What is it?'

I told him. 'Can't hurt,' he said. 'Cut along home, Dr Mac,' he told me. 'See you in the morning.'

Florence was asleep in a chair outside her mother's room. I didn't wake her.

3rd February

When I got home to my own house, Mum was lying asleep in her bed, Dad was asleep beside her on the other camp bed and Uncle Donald was sitting on the porch in his shirtsleeves.

'How are they, Charlotte?'

'Mrs Reilly's through the worst but I don't know about Mrs Barnes.' I came and sat beside him. Albie was wrapped up, nestling against Uncle Donald so I took the other side and he put his arm around me.

'Poor overworked fairy,' he said. 'I thought I'd save you some trouble, and then I give you a lot more.'

'No,' I said. 'Because you got sick, Dad got well. I think you might have saved all of us. Tell me a story,' I said. Suddenly I felt like a child again and I wanted to be distracted.

'You're a caution,' said Uncle Donald. 'A fairy story or a true story?'

'A true story,' I said.

In the warm dark he started to speak. His voice was soft.

'We were all lined up in the desert,' he said. 'Forty thousand of us. We were clearing a way for Allenby's march to Jerusalem, so we had to secure the wells. That's the important thing in deserts, Charlotte; whoever has the water rules the land. The horses were thirsty and so were we. We were on short rations, pint a day for a man and three pints for a horse. That ain't enough for any neddy.

'We all lined up, each rider knee to knee with the next, in the dark. I was riding beside my mate Eddy. All you could hear was the soft clopping of hoofs on sand and the jingle of the bridles and the creaking of the saddles. The sun came up and I looked left and right and there we were, a fine sight, Charlotte, us with our feathered hats and the horses all moving at a trot. We would have made a fine target, too, for anyone with a big gun.

'Then my mate, Eddy, said to me, "They have broke the wells of Beersheba," and I thought it sounded just like something out of the Bible. He could smell water, see, country-bred bloke, Eddy, nose like an anteater. Then the heads went up, because the horses had smelled it too, and we were off. It was like a race. They smelled water and they were going to get it and no one could have stopped the charge to Beersheba, Charlotte, no one. I reckon we was supposed to wait for orders but the horses had bolted and on we went. We raced across that desert as though we were trying to win the Melbourne Cup.

'And it worked. The poor Turks had their guns sighted for distance and they didn't know what we were when this huge dust cloud boiled out of the dawn. By the time they worked out what we were, we were on them. Eddy says he saw a Turk's face, absolutely stonkered, as we jumped the gun pits and were into Beersheba.

'Next thing I remember was falling off into a well. Somewhere along the line someone had stuck a bayonet into my thigh. Never even felt it. We had Beersheba. The horses had as much water as they could drink, and our general had his victory. And that's a dead secret, Charlotte. No one else must ever know that the last, greatest cavalry charge in history started because the horses bolted.'

'Is that true?' I asked, and yawned.

'Fair dinkum,' said Uncle Donald. 'Off to bed, Charlotte.'

And true or not, I've written it all down.

8th February

Doctor Barnes thinks we are coming through the flu, though it is bad in the Eastern Suburbs now. Mrs Barnes is better, though still lying in her bed, and Mrs Reilly is up and back in the kitchen, helped by her sons. Uncle Donald is putting on weight and even Mum gets up for four hours a day. I've been doing the doctor's rounds every night. Bethesda knows me now. Last few nights Dad has come with me, to make sure that no one offers me any insult, but no one has. My cap and apron make me not a sheila, as Curly said, but a nurse.

Mr Lee and his sons said goodbye, gave me another bunch of herbs, and caught the train for Geelong. They had dismantled their tent and taken everything with them, all packed together into a knapsack. Faro was still weak but he was walking. They just had to go over the crossing to get to the station. All that remained of their being there was a rectangle of dried grass.

'Remember,' Mr Lee said to me. 'Star of destiny. Plain as plain,' he added, hefted the tent, and walked away.

'What was that about?' said Dad.

'He read my hand,' I told him. 'He said I'd be what I wanted to be. And I want to be a doctor,' I said.

Dad thought about this. A few months ago he would just have told me not to be a silly girl. But this was my new dad. Bethesda stopped outside the Thomas house.

Dad watched as I talked to old Mrs Thomas, gave some more of the blue mixture to young Mrs Thomas and told Mr Thomas that he was over the worst and ought to be thinking cheerful thoughts and helping his mother. He told me that he had already been to Sunday School and knew that. Flu patients get irritable.

Then we called on Miss Jones, who was sitting up, planning the menu for her wedding reception. Her mother said that her young man had also survived. She said she'd send the doctor and me an invitation to the wedding.

When we were back in the cart Dad said, 'You'd have to go to school.'

'I know, and I know I can't. But I'll be a nurse, and then when I get my trust money, I'll go back to school and then I'll go to university. And then I'll be a doctor.'

Usually Dad forbids all mention of the trust money and I expected him to be cross. But he asked. Now he seemed thoughtful.

'Did I do wrong,' he asked, 'refusing to take Alice's money?'

'I don't know,' I said. 'You didn't know you'd come back hurt from the war. It probably seemed like the right thing to do at the time.'

'Pride,' he said. Then he quoted the Bible. '"Pride goeth before a fall."'

Then he sat without speaking while we called at the Warrell's. She was well.

Then at the Kerr's, where Mr Kerr was incoherent with relief. 'It worked,' he said. 'I played that Caruso record until I could have smashed it myself. I gave her drinks with red pepper in. Nothing happened, until suddenly, this morning, she opened her eyes and said, "William, for God's sake don't play that again," so I played it again, and she actually sat up and then was very sick and now her fever's dropped, I could swear.'

It had, indeed, dropped to normal. Mrs Kerr was still very cross with her husband but she accepted some beef tea and I thought she would recover. I told Mr Kerr to keep the Caruso record in reserve in case she floated away again. She glared at me, which was a good sign.

At Matty's house her mother was recovered. I left some of the blue mixture. All of the children were healthy. Matty said that Curly came every day and he had promised to take her mother dancing when she got better and he got the cast off his leg. She likes Curly. The smallest child is already calling him 'Daddy'. So that is what Doctor was chuckling about.

At the boarding house, Dad went for a beer with the soldiers while I did the rounds. No one was worse and most of them were recovering. The landlady was up and sitting in her parlour. Some furniture had survived the soldiers' cleaning efforts.

I asked her how she felt.

'Much better,' she said. 'Really much better. Better than I've felt in years. I should have thrown that oilcloth away years ago, taken down all that filthy, torn lace at the windows. I've asked the chaps to do some work around the house. Fine fellows, those soldiers. I always was partial to a soldier, in my youth. Truth is, my dear, my husband died and I just rolled myself into a ball and got bitter.'

Nothing like a brush with death to make people appreciate being alive, Doctor says. She looked quite different. Cleaner, for a start. And she sounded different.

I went out to the garden to find Dad. He was sitting on the veranda with Billo, Thommo, Owen and Bruce.

'Yair, we're goin' into the paintin' and decoratin' line,' said Owen. 'The old chook wants us to kalsomime her walls and give the old place a bit of a spruce up. If we can spruce this place up we can do it to anything. What are you goin' to do, mate?'

'My brother-in-law has an idea about a business,' said Dad. 'Don't know what it is, though.'

'If Don says it's a good idea, then it'll be a good idea,' said Owen. 'Nice to see you back on your pins, Alec! Thought you were a goner, I did.'

'So did I,' said Dad. 'But I wasn't.'

'Good on yer! Hello, Miss Mac,' said Owen. 'How's the sick list?'

'Looking better,' I said.

'And what are you going to do after the flu's over, Miss Mac?' asked Owen.

'She's going to be a doctor,' said Dad. I gasped, but the soldiers seemed to approve.

'Good on yer,' said Owen.

16th February

We're at Geelong! Once Mum could get up for a reasonable time, Doctor Barnes packed us all off on a holiday. Mrs Reilly is going to look after Sable and the chooks. We took Florence with us. Her mother is recovering slowly and Dr Barnes said he could do without his assistant because the flu is really dying down in the western suburbs. He says that it's been caught by everyone who was going to catch it, and now it was off looking for nice fresh blood.

Disease knows no barriers. No justice. No fairness. No mercy. It cannot be reasoned with. It must be fought. And I am going to fight it.

We're staying in a nice old house almost on the shore and we go walking every day. I didn't say anything to Dad about what he said—about me being a doctor. I wondered if he meant it. It might have been a joke. And for me it was too serious for joking.

We went for a swim this morning. I couldn't help noticing Uncle Donald's scar. It's an ugly, lumpy curved line all down his chest and belly. It must have almost gutted him, as he said. He's still weak and coughing but Dad has put on weight and he looks taller and stronger. When they went running into the sea, it was Dad carrying Albie on his back, not Uncle Donald.

I waited until we were all sitting in our favourite shelter, a gazebo in the gardens, before I asked Dad, 'Did you mean it?'

'Mean what?' he asked, but he was teasing.

'Me being a doctor.'

'You have a trust fund,' he said. 'If you want to go to school and then to university, you need to convince your trustees that it is a good investment.'

'My trustees?' I imagined stern men in suits, somewhere in the city. 'Who are my trustees?'

'Well, there's me,' said Uncle Donald, pushing back his hat.

'And there's me,' said Mum.

They all laughed, but I didn't.

'Will you let me go to school with Florence and then pay my fees at the university, if I can get in?' I asked.

Mum looked concerned. 'Are you sure?' she asked. 'It means years of study, no pretty clothes, no dances, no boy friends . . .'

'Mum!' I exclaimed, embarrassed.

'She means it,' said Uncle Donald. 'She doesn't care about pretty clothes, she doesn't care about boy friends. She's only on this holiday because the doctor made her go.'

'Oh, Charlotte! You can come to school with me!' Florence was delighted and hugged me directly. 'I didn't want to go without you!'

'Very well,' said Mum.

'Shake,' said Uncle Donald.

I shook his hand and then I hugged him. Then I hugged Mum. And Dad. And Florence, Amelia and Albie all demanded hugs as well.

Then we bought ice-cream. I felt very happy. I wasn't expecting to be happy again after Lily was taken. But she would have been pleased by her gravestone. It was of pink granite, with her own name and dates and a carved lily.

I still miss her. I suppose I always will. But my family is back together, and Dad is setting up in business with Uncle Donald when everyone is well enough.

'Horses are finished,' said Uncle Donald, not without regret. He really loves horses. 'Motor cars are the coming thing. And if you have motor cars, what do you need? You need garages! You need repair shops! You need petrol stations! I tell you, Alec, we can make a good living out of the motor car.'

I don't like them, dirty noisy things, and where's the motor car which will bring you home again, fast asleep, like Bethesda brings Doctor Barnes home? But Uncle and Dad are very excited about it.

'What if . . . what if I get taken by the old trouble?' asked Dad, very quietly.

'What if I never get any healthier than this?' asked Uncle Donald. 'We're both crocks now, old man. We'll manage.'

I linked arms with Amelia and Florence. Mum walked with Uncle Donald, Albie and Dad. The flu epidemic was a terrible thing. But like Uncle says about wars, sometimes terrible things have good results.

When we go home again, I will go back to school, and then I will become a doctor. Mr Lee said I would be what I want to be, and I shall.

Historical notes

The Influenza Pandemic of 1918–19 killed 27 million people worldwide, double the number who died in the Great War. It killed 5,000 people in Victoria and about 13,000 in Australia. Most of the deaths were in the cities of Sydney and Melbourne. It was a very peculiar disease. Instead of killing the very young and the very old, it killed the healthiest and the strongest. Most of the flu deaths were of people between the age of 15 and 40. It killed about 8 per cent of the people infected.

The New South Wales Government issued a proclamation in January 1919 which began: "To the People of New South Wales. A danger greater than war faces the State . . . and threatens the lives of all. Each day the progress of the battle is published in the press. Watch out for it. Follow the advice given and the battle can be won. From today . . . EVERYONE SHALL WEAR A MASK."

The flu wore itself out by about July 1919, after which the racetracks, music halls, pubs, schools and churches were re-opened. At its peak it is estimated that about 60 per cent of all Australians had the flu. There was no effective treatment. Patients who were nursed, by whatever method, either lived or died. Those who were not nursed died. Many nurses mentioned the strange, toxic smell, like wet mice, which they thought might have come from thousands of men living in filthy trenches for years, making some sort of infectious poison in their bodies. Church ladies, council workers and many ordinary people were the heroes of the flu epidemic, working all hours, making soup, tending the sick, keeping shops open and driving wagons and trains.

The virus has recently been retrieved from bodies buried in permafrost. It was a chance mutation between human and animal flu, for people who survived the 1919 pandemic had antibodies for an animal disease called swine fever.

It could happen again. This time it would travel by jet, not by troop ship. The World Health Organisation has a disaster plan should another Spanish Flu come along, because there are a lot more people in the world now, and the flu would move much faster.

The First World War

At the time it was known as the Great War or just the War, because the soldiers expected never to fight another one. It began when Germany invaded Belgium on the 4th of August 1914. England then declared war on Germany. New Zealand and Australia eagerly rushed into training, forming the Australian New Zealand Army Corps (ANZAC) who were later sent to Gallipoli and martyrdom on hot cliffs.

The war quickly bogged down into trenches. Neither side could advance very far. The soldiers would pour out of a trench, 'over the top', and would be cut down by machine guns and left to die in the space between the trenches, 'no man's land', so it was safer not to move.

The Light Horse took part in the last great cavalry charge (cavalry now ride in tanks, not on horses) and it is said that their horses bolted, smelling water.

The Great War dragged on, brutal and slow and murderous, for four years. The life expectancy of a new soldier on the battlefront at the Somme was twenty minutes. There were some bright patches. Even today the schoolchildren at Villers-Brettoneux have a sign on their school that says 'Never Forget the Australians'. The people were deeply grateful that the Australian soldiers should come so far from their home to defend them and they have never forgotten their courage. The Australians were considered excellent troops but cheeky, insolent, insubordinate and occasionally unwilling to carry out some order which they considered ridiculous.

The War seemed endless. Finally two things happened. Sir John Monash (Australia) managed to convince Lloyd George, the British Prime Minister, to attack trenches using tanks, not men, and the Americans finally committed troops. They only fought one action but they represented a huge pool of soldiers and supplies yet untouched. The Germans then realised that they could not win and fell back, fighting bravely, to Germany, where the blockade of all of their trade had produced a famine. In the meantime, their navy mutinied and the Kaiser, their head of state, was overthrown in a coup by people hungry, cold, and utterly sick of war.

The Great War proved nothing and killed 59,342 Australians and wounded 152,171 out of a population of just over four million. It had a devastating impact on the post War economy. Many of the wounded could not work, and many of them had shell shock, which is now called Post Traumatic Stress Disorder. It was not understood at the time and there was no effective treatment.

On 1919

Most houses in the inner suburbs were sewered and had running water. The only way to get hot water was to light the copper, a big cauldron with a fire underneath. Cooking was by means of a slow combustion stove, though up-to-date houses had gas cookers and were lit by electricity. There were very few telephones. The motor car was around but only rich people had one and most people travelled by foot, bicycle, horse-drawn bus or steam train.

During the War many women had worked at trades which had only been done by men—driving trains, mining coal, fighting fires, working as chemists and clerks and accountants and practising medicine. There were no women lawyers and few women doctors.

For all but a few who could afford the fees, school finished at intermediate, year ten, when most boys found a job or an apprenticeship and most girls worked at home or in shops and factories until they married. Very few married women worked. Female teachers and public servants were not allowed to work after they married. For a wife to have to work meant that the man of the house was a failure.

References

The best book about the Influenza Pandemic of 1918–19 is *The Plague of the Spanish Lady* by Richard Collier, Macmillan, London, 1974, though please note that Australia got the flu January to July 1919.

On Australian soldiers in the Great War, read C E W Bean *Anzac to Amiens*, Australian War Memorial, Canberra, 1961.

KERRY GREENWOOD

Kerry Greenwood has written nineteen novels and has worked as a folk-singer, a factory hand, a director, a producer, an editor, a translator, a costume-maker, a cook, and also qualified as a solicitor. She is an honorary Greek. She is a historian. She works part time for Victoria Legal Aid as an advocate in Magistrates' Courts and is currently working on her twelfth Phryne Fisher book and *Stormbringer*, a huge science fiction novel. She has written four science fiction novels for young adults: *The Broken Wheel* (which won the Aurealis Award in 1996), *Cave Rats*, *Whaleroad* and *Feral*.

She is not married, has no children and lives with four cats and an accredited wizard. In her spare time she stares blankly out of the window.

And she has no idea where she gets her ideas from.